CHANGE THE NAME

CHANGE
THE NAME

ANNA KAVAN

PETER OWEN

London & Chester Springs PA

PETER OWEN LIMITED
73 Kenway Road London SW5 0RE
Peter Owen Books are distributed in the USA by
Dufour Editions Inc. Chester Springs PA 19425–0449

First published in Great Britain 1941
Published in this edition 1993
© The Estate of Anna Kavan 1941, 1993

ISBN 1–7206–0883–X

A catalogue record for this book is available
from the British Library

Printed and made in Great Britain

ONE

In the year of Our Lord nineteen-hundred-and-twelve all senior schoolgirls wore their hair either plaited or 'tied back'. On a certain winter morning the hair of Celia Henzell, confined at the back of her neck by a bow of stiff black ribbon, was far the brightest thing in the school garden. Not very long, wavy, thick and vigorous looking, fair with a faint chestnut burnish, it gave her the appearance of being accompanied by a private sunbeam as, wearing an old navy blue coat and the regulation black goloshes, she walked quickly between the evergreens and the empty flower-beds under the dour Midland sky. Behind her was the wooden gymnasium where the upper forms had just been rehearsing the end of term play which they were to present in a few days' time. A short distance ahead was the school itself, Saint Ermins, a large, nondescript, ivy-covered mansion built as a country residence for some wealthy Birmingham manufacturer about thirty years earlier. A damp gravel path led from the gym to the side entrance of the school used by the girls. The front drive, fringed in shaggy cypresses, seldom used except by visitors and the arriving or departing station flies at the beginning and end of term, was on the left. At one end the drive terminated in the double-doored main entrance of Saint Ermins; at the other, in a high, blank, conventual wooden gate on the outside of which was a brass plate bearing the old-fashioned wording 'school for the daughters of gentlemen'.

Five years' familiarity with these surroundings had long since deprived them of objectivity in the eyes of

Celia Henzell. Nevertheless, on this dull winter morning, her blue eyes did actually focus with conscious recognition for a moment, a slightly troubled look appeared fugitively on her pale, clear, rather neutral face. Extraordinary to think that this was her last term at Saint Ermins. Incredible that soon she would be treading for the last time this weedy path upon which she had trodden so many hundred times. It was not that she was particularly devoted to the school; but the thought of leaving it was accompanied by a painful anxiety about the future, an uncertainty so odious that for a second or two she stopped dead beside a clump of glossy-leaved laurels.

Then the worried suggestion vanished from her face. By a quite unchildlike trick that was characteristic of her she changed the expression of her eyes, unfocusing them, and seeming with their altered gaze to have changed the whole trend of her thoughts. She walked on again. Her lips began to move soundlessly, repeating some of the words of the recent rehearsal. 'Cromwell, I charge thee, fling away ambition. By this sin fell the angels. How then can man, the image of his Maker, hope to gain by it?'

Suddenly there was a noise of scuffling footsteps, a small girl of about twelve years old came flying round the laurel bushes, colliding with Celia Henzell and almost falling over backwards as a result of the impact. The senior grasped her shoulder to steady her.

'Marjorie, you silly little idiot! Why don't you look where you're going? And what are you doing out here, anyway, when you ought to be in class?' Celia's voice was pleasant to hear. It was a low-pitched voice, singularly melodious for that of a young girl, and it pronounced words distinctly and without any trace of accent or affectation.

8

The child wriggled in her hold, cocked her head like a cheeky young bird, and replied: 'Miss Rowe sent me out to find you. She wants you in her study.'

'Then why couldn't you say so at once?' Celia exclaimed, releasing her so impetuously that she nearly overbalanced again.

Unconscious of the astonished stare of the messenger whom she had already forgotten, the elder girl fled in the direction of the school. At last it had come, the summons for which she had been waiting for several days. At last she was to know the best or the worst about her future fate. In the dark, inconvenient cloakroom that smelt of mackintoshes and soapy wash-basins, she dragged off her coat and goloshes. It was typical of Celia Henzell that even in her excitement the motions of her hands were direct, methodical and precise.

No special qualifications were expected of the heads of small private schools during the epoch˜when Miss Rowe decided to enter the scholastic world. She had received a legacy on the death of her parents and, because she was fond of girls, she had used the money to set herself up as headmistress of Saint Ermins. Instead of degrees and diplomas she had a certain knack of managing children and adolescents and of winning their confidence. She did not herself teach any subject except Scripture; but the Scripture classes were conducted with such thoroughness and enthusiasm that to most of the pupils of Saint Ermins the history of the Israelites was far more vividly familiar than that of their own country. The school always obtained a record number of certificates in the periodic diocesan examinations.

Miss Rowe's study was the pleasantest room in the building. In spite of the stationery cupboards and the big, businesslike desk, it still looked more like the study of a private house than a room in a school. This cold morning a good fire was burning in the grate and the air was comfortably warm. A fine pink azalea covered with bloom stood on a table near the window.

The headmistress sat at her desk with a pile of exercise books beside her. Spare and flat-chested, she was one of those women whose appearance alter little between the ages of thirty and sixty. Impossible to imagine her as a young girl, it was equally hard to visualize her as a very old woman. The pile of green-covered books with which she was occupied were the 'best books' belonging to the third form who had been told to write an account of the fall of Jericho. Miss Rowe finished reading the page before her and unscrewed the fountain-pen which she wore in a leather sheath attached to her waistband. From the broad gold nib the letters flowed smoothly, black, plain and rounded. 'Fair,' she wrote at the foot of the page, 'but the handwriting is slovenly.' She drew a condemnatory circle round a faultily-erased blot, paused for a moment's consideration, and then added the marks 'Six out of ten'.

There was a knock at the door. 'That will be Celia Henzell,' thought the mistress. Her face seemed to grow more angular as she called out 'Come in!'

The interview before her was distasteful, and although she was not the sort of woman to shrink from an unpleasant task she would be glad when it was over. She replaced the cap of her fountain-pen. But instead of putting the pen away in its leather case, she continued to hold it poised between her fingers with their spatulate, well-trimmed nails. How the time flew! It seemed only the other day that Celia was one of the 'little ones' in the second form and now she was leaving school and almost grown up. That was the worst part about keeping a school. Girls came to you for several years so that you got to know them really well, got really fond of them, and then, just at the most interesting period of their lives, off they went, and most likely you never even saw them again.

Not that she would feel especially the loss of Celia who had never been one of her particular favourites like Doris Rushton or little Molly Treherne. But her departure would mean the disappearance of yet another familiar face. A striking looking girl she had grown into, too, with that brilliant hair and that alabaster complexion: certainly not pretty, but unusual — striking, in fact, was exactly the right word. She looked the sort of girl whose life would be out of the ordinary; who would not easily settle down to the conventional middle-class routine of marriage, children and housekeeping. A great pity that her father was so set against her going to the university.

All these thoughts passed through the mind of the woman in the severe, high-collared blouse during the infinitesimal fraction of time which elapsed between Celia's entrance and the first words being spoken between them.

'You sent for me, Miss Rowe? You've heard from father?'

'Yes, Celia. I had a letter from your father this morning and I'm afraid it means a disappointment for you.'

The rare animation that had given life to the girl's face died as abruptly as if a sponge had wiped it away. Her expression at once returned to its rather baffling neutrality which at the same time touched the headmistress and faintly antagonized her. She appreciated the bitterness of the blow to Celia's hopes, but why must the girl put on that inaccessible, stubborn look, as if she would rather die than make any display of feeling? Just because she had never been able to feel real affection for this one of her pupils, the warm-hearted Miss Rowe laid aside her pen, got up and went across to where Celia was standing.

'Come over to the fire for a minute,' she said kindly, taking her by the hand.

They moved, and stood together in front of the cheerful flames; the mistress unhappy because she was obliged to inflict pain, the girl not exactly ungracious, but unresponsive, her cold hand limp in the other's clasp.

'I'm sorry about this, Celia; more sorry than I can say.

But I'm afraid there's nothing more I can do to help you. I wrote to your father as I promised and told him that it was my opinion and the opinion of all the staff here that you would do well at Oxford. I told him that our English mistress considered that you had a real talent for writing and that some of your essays had been quite remarkable. I put forward my personal recommendation that, if it were at all possible, you should be allowed to continue your studies and finally to take a degree in English.' Miss Rowe paused and gazed at the young, non-committal, partly averted face.

'She's waiting for me to say something,' Celia thought. 'Why can't she let me go now? What's the use of trying to be nice about it?'

'And what did father answer?' she said aloud to the fire, in a flat tone.

'He said he couldn't afford to send you to Oxford.'

'Oh, but that's simply not true! Father's got plenty of money.'

Miss Rowe withdrew her hand. She had wanted the girl to show some feeling, and now she had certainly done so. But it was the wrong sort of feeling, and the head-mistress felt herself stiffening.

'Really, Celia, I can't allow you to speak of your father in that way.'

'But, Miss Rowe, it's so unjust! If my brother had lived he would have gone to Oxford as a matter of course — if I'd been a boy I'd have gone. It's just because I'm a girl that father thinks it isn't worth while spending any-thing on my brains — '

The elder woman frowned and looked down at the plain gold pin that fastened her dark green tie. Her sympathetic feelings were rapidly giving way to disapproving

13

ones. It would have been better if the girl had kept silent than to have her breaking out in this way, in spite of the disquieting element of truth in what she said. Of course, there was no getting away from the fact that fathers did not give their daughters equal chances with their sons. It seemed all wrong, but what was the good of running one's head against a brick wall? And, after all, a system that had lasted for so many centuries must have some fundamental justification. The unelastic and not very intelligent mind of the headmistress was incapable of surmounting that brick wall of tradition.

'I can make allowances for your disappointment,' she said precisely. 'I realize that this is a blow to you. But you must understand clearly that I do not countenance for a moment any spirit of criticism or wilful rebellion against your father's decision. Perhaps when you are at home you may be able to talk to him yourself and persuade him to change his mind.'

'I'm afraid there's no chance of that. I've often tried to persuade him before and it's never been any good. If your letter couldn't influence him nothing I could say would have any effect.'

Miss Rowe observed with relief that Celia had reverted to her usual restrained attitude. Evidently she had got over the first shock and was going to take her disappointment philosophically. With the end of the uncongenial interview in sight, the principal's eye wandered almost affectionately towards the pile of exercise books on the desk. Thank goodness, she would be free in a moment or two now to get back to the familiar work which she really enjoyed.

'In that case, Celia, you must simply put the idea out of your head,' she said briskly, 'and make up your mind to living at home. After all, that's what most girls do when they leave school until they get married.'

'I shall marry the first man who asks me, whether I like him or not,' said Celia in a matter-of-fact tone.

Miss Rowe glanced at her sharply.

'I hope you will do nothing so wrong or so foolish,' she remarked in her most pedagogic voice, now definitely antagonized by her pupil. She was aware, as she spoke, of a curious illusion. Just for a second, it seemed to her that she had seen the face before her, not as it was now, the face of a seventeen-year-old schoolgirl, but as it would be in ten or twelve or fifteen years time, the smooth, secretive countenance of a mature and determined woman.

The illusion, fantastic as it was, had a disturbing effect on the headmistress which did not immediately vanish when she was left alone. Feeling suddenly put out and slightly liverish, she sat down at her desk again and altered the marks on the open book from 'Six out of ten' to 'Five out of ten'.

FREDERICK HENZELL, solicitor and town clerk of the quiet old Midland borough of Jessington, had only once in his life made a speculation. This was when, as a young married man, he had decided to invest some of his patrimony in real estate.

It was during the late Victorian period of prosperity when many successful business men were buying homes in such places as Jessington which were still unspoiled and yet within easy reach of the great manufacturing centres. Desborough House, on the outskirts of the town, was just the sort of residence that might be expected to appeal to a family man of comfortable, moderate means. A large grey stone house with a turret at one corner, it was situated midway along a road of similar large, newish, rather gloomy, rather pretentious houses, set a good distance apart with gardens sloping down at the back to the sluggish river, Jess. The original owner of the property died suddenly, the relatives were anxious for a quick settlement of the estate, and Frederick Henzell was able to buy at a reasonable figure. He was in no great hurry for a re-sale: he had only to bide his time and there seemed no doubt that he would realize a substantial profit on the transaction. It looked as if the young lawyer was on to a safe thing.

But by one of those incalculable chances which bring confusion upon speculators, Desborough House unaccountably failed to sell. All around Jessington people were buying houses almost exactly similar in size, situation and style. Only Desborough House obstinately and incomprehensibly remained empty.

Prosperous gentlemen came with their wives and inspected the long drawing-room with its fashionably adjacent conservatory, the spacious, inconvenient kitchen premises, the lofty bedrooms and the unheatable passages. They walked round the lawns and shrubberies of the orderly garden and admired the view of the brownish, slow-moving stream. They asked questions and entered into negotiations which somehow never got beyond the preliminary stages. Then they went away and bought property elsewhere.

As time passed and still no purchaser appeared, Mr. Henzell began to grow anxious. He had talked a little about his speculation at the start, and now it seemed to him that people were beginning to smile covertly whenever the subject came up. Probably he imagined most of the smiles: he was a dignified, staid young man who could not tolerate even a hint of ridicule.

Desborough House gradually became a sort of nightmare to him. It was a white elephant, a millstone about his neck, a horrible deadweight of loss which would cripple him to the end of his days. In the evenings, when he was unlikely to meet any of his acquaintances, he would go to look at the house, letting himself in furtively through the padlocked gates like a criminal drawn irresistibly to the scene of his crime. He would prowl round the paths, scowling at the building which stood there wan and vacant in the dusk, a huge, hideously substantial spectre, the concrete sign of his failure. Every now and then he fancied that a new crack or a fresh patch of damp had appeared on the walls. It was doing the house no good to remain empty all this time. Besides the inevitable small fabric deteriorations, a vaguely unfavourable reputation was slowly attaching itself to the place. In the insidious way that such things happen, Desborough House was becoming known as unsaleable. Suddenly Frederick Henzell came to a decision. He would live in Desborough House himself until it was sold.

With his wife and his two young children, the solicitor moved out of the little Georgian house in the middle of the town, the home which was the right size for his small family and conveniently close to his office, and took up residence in the large, inappropriate, rather forbidding house on the banks of the Jess. He told Marion Henzell that it was only a temporary measure. The fiction was kept up between them that one day the house would be sold. Nevertheless, both husband and wife were convinced in their secret hearts that this was to be their permanent abode, and the move had a profound effect upon each of them.

The unfortunate outcome of his solitary speculation caused the lawyer to become obsessed by the need for economy. Right up to the time of his death, years after conscientious saving had made good his original loss, he insisted on maintaining a frugal and even parsimonious mode of life. His never very open nature hardened into a cautious self-sufficiency. Towards his family he behaved with a kind of automatic, preoccupied politeness that was rather devastating. His heart was not with them but with his work. All his interests centred in the little dark panelled office that was his real home. His professional associates respected him as a man of sound judgment and integrity. He made no friends and few enemies. Without being exactly unsociable, he clearly preferred his own company to that of others, and when he did

appear in public his manner was stiff and uncompromising—
perhaps, too, rather dull. Nobody knew much about him
except that he was a reliable lawyer, a good husband, and
the owner of a house which no one wanted to buy. Presumably there was nothing more to know.

The influence of Desborough House upon Mrs.
Henzell was deplorable from the beginning. The young
wife bitterly regretted the loss of her comfortable little
home near the shops and the life of the town. In this cold,
dismal barn of a place with half the rooms locked and
unfurnished, struggling along with two servants where
six were needed, she felt shut off from everything that
was friendly and familiar. She was a docile woman and
she did not complain much or fight against circumstances.
But as she moved about the chilly rooms or walked
through the flowerless garden which exhaled already an
inexplicable aura of melancholy discouragement, she
often sighed to herself and sometimes her pale blue eyes
filled with tears. Frederick said that they must watch
every penny and she obediently set herself to the task of
economizing. But the struggle was too much for her; she
began to lose heart and to retire more and more into herself. Each month it became increasingly hard for her to
make the effort of going into the town. It seemed less and
less worth while changing her clothes and smartening
herself up to go shopping or visiting her friends. She
began to suffer from headaches. Her figure lost its agreeable contours, her hair, which had been her main beauty,
lost its colour and gloss, her face lost its smoothness and
acquired fretful lines. At thirty she was already starting
to look old. Her husband appeared not to notice any
alteration in her. Absorbed in his private world, funda-
mentally uninterested in human relationships, perhaps

the lawyer really was unaware that his wife was gradually dropping out of everything and developing into a hypochondriac.

When the elder child, Harold, died of pneumonia at the age of thirteen, Desborough House became definitely and permanently a house of mourning. Marion Henzell kept her son's room exactly as he had left it and planted ivy from his grave under her bedroom window. The spirit of the dead boy seemed to brood in the cold passages, to roam disconsolately through the damp garden, and to pervade the whole place with a vague atmosphere of frustration and sadness.

ELECTRICITY had not been installed at Desborough House. In the dining-room the gas fitting over the table was partially concealed by a faded red silk frill through which the light shed an uneven flush upon the faces of the three diners. Beyond the lighted island of table the big room swam in deep sanguinary shade, looking, with its dark crimson papered walls, like the setting for a grotesque tableau of Jonah in the belly of the whale. The air was exceedingly cold, smelling slightly of fish-cakes and slightly of the paraffin used in the ugly black oil stove which stood in the empty fireplace and was supposed to take off the chill of the winter night.

Old Mattie, who had served the Henzells for nearly twenty years, came treading heavily up to the table in her shapeless black strapped shoes, and deposited a dish of fruit in front of her master. The meal was at an end.

The lawyer lifted the dish containing two apples, two oranges and a banana, and offered it to his wife and daughter, both of whom declined the dessert. He helped himself to an apple and started to peel it. In the silence, Mattie's retreating footsteps could be distinctly heard, plodding ponderously down the stone-floored passage that led to the kitchen.

No one spoke in the dining-room. The master of the house sat peeling his apple, his head fringed in close-cut grey hair slightly bent, his imperturbable, repressive face with its small clipped moustache fixed in concentrated yet absent attention over the trivial task which his fingers performed so meticulously. A tiny sigh escaped the woman seated opposite him as the long reddish curl of rind finally fell unbroken on to his plate. Mrs. Henzell was unaware both of the sigh and of the fact that her own nervous attention was fastened upon her husband. Wrapped in a thick woollen jacket with a cashmere shawl over her shoulders, she looked shrivelled and small, more like the grandmother than the mother of the bright-haired girl who sat passively with her hands folded in her lap.

The lawyer was cutting the apple into sections with a silver knife, closing his jaws with a slight snap upon each mouthful, and masticating the hard fruit with a crunching sound.

'I hear that the council has decided to cut down two of the elms in Tilbury Gardens,' he remarked conversationally.

'Have they really? What a pity! Such lovely old trees . . .' Marion Henzell had a quick, twittering voice that often trailed into indistinct incoherence at the end of a sentence, leaving the hearer with a sense of uncertainty that could be both exasperating and distressing.

'It's high time they came down. They're getting dangerous,' returned her husband.

There was another long pause. Mr. Henzell finished his apple, rolled his table napkin into its silver ring and laid it beside his plate. Something — her prolonged silence, perhaps — caused him to glance at his daughter. She had hardly spoken a word throughout the meal. The lawyer was conscious of this, but the consciousness did not disturb him. To-night, as always, he had played the part which politeness required of him in introducing topics of conversation. If Celia preferred not to respond that was her affair. The emotions behind her lack of response did not concern him, nor did it occur to him to wonder what they might be.

He was absolutely without curiosity as to what went on in the minds of his family. He asked no more of them than that they should behave in the same decorous manner which he himself always maintained. Their private feelings and thoughts were of no interest to him. Nevertheless, an almost imperceptible breath ruffled the ocean of his composure as he looked at the tall, expressionless girl. In spite of the fact that she was so quiet and apparently acquiescent, there was something extraordinarily positive about her, some curiously potent emanation of character that, even when she was not asserting herself in any way, penetrated his up-till-now impregnable preoccupation and made him aware of her presence. The atmosphere of the house had changed in some way since she had come back from Saint Ermins; it seemed to have become a fraction of a degree less placid. 'I hope she's not going to be difficult,' was the thought which formed itself in the lawyer's mind. But the thought was banished almost before it was registered. Preposterous, even for a moment, to anticipate trouble from such a source! Frederick Henzell rose from the table, extinguished the oil stove, and opened the door for his womenfolk.

If the dining-room had been cold, the totally unheated hall was arctic. The black and white tiles rang like slabs of ice under foot, breath steamed frostily in the air.

Celia made for a door on the left leading to an anteroom where she kept her books and personal possessions. She rarely sat with her parents in the evening. The anteroom, like the hall, was unheated; but when her father and Mattie were out of the way she would re-light the oil lamp and take it in with her. The girl, no more than her elders, thought it strange that the daughter of the house should sit apart, alone in an unwarmed room. It was a thing to be taken for granted, the custom of Desborough House; and she preferred it so.

THE solicitor followed his wife into their usual sitting-room, the study, the only room in the house where there was a fire. The drawing-room was far too large to be economically heated, and a fire was only lighted there on Sundays when it was allowed to burn for a few hours for the purpose of airing the room. By contrast with the rest of the house the study felt hot, even stuffy. Frederick Henzell did not like the temperature of a room to rise above sixty degrees, but he put up with the warmth out of consideration for Marion's tastes. He would not have dreamed of suggesting that a window be opened although the close atmosphere was really disagreeable to him. In any case he would not have to endure it for long. The white marble clock on the mantelpiece struck a sharp *ping* under its glass dome. Half-past eight. At nine o'clock Mattie would bring in the cup of Benger's Food which Mrs. Henzell drank every night before going to bed. This was his signal for departure. He would say good-night, fetch his hat, overcoat and stick, and stroll down to the Conservative Club to smoke a pipe, look at the papers, and perhaps exchange a few words on municipal matters with one of his colleagues.

Marion Henzell responded at once to the warmth of the study. She discarded her shawl, touched with her fingers the thin, faded hair which encircled her forehead in an untidy roll, and looked several years younger than she had done in the dining-room. In the unshaded, unflattering gas-light it was now possible to detect traces of a vanished prettiness in her pinched face.

She sat down by the fire in a chair covered in some carpet-like fabric with a design of brown flowers on a mustard ground. On the arm of the chair hung a large velvet bag from which she extracted a bundle of light grey knitting. Mr. Henzell sat opposite her, unfolding *The Times* which he had already seen at breakfast that day. With the hand not occupied by the newspaper he patted the outside of his pocket to make sure that his tobacco pouch and pipe were in it. He never smoked in his wife's presence, but he would have a pipe on his way to the club later on.

The airless room was not pleasing to any aesthetic sense. It was full of unbeautiful objects arranged in what appeared to be a haphazard way. Clearly the occupants of the house either lacked the gift or the initiative for what is called 'home making'. The furniture had obviously been chosen for a different room and no attempt had been made to adjust it to its present surroundings. The clock ticked: the gas hissed on steadily. The paper rustled: the wool whispered over the needles. A covered bird made small, uneasy scratching sounds in its draped cage. Now and then a coal collapsed with a noise like a smothered cough as the big fire burned lower.

Just as the hands of the clock indicated eight minutes to nine the rhythm of small domestic sounds was interrupted. There was a step in the hall; the door started to open. Both the seated figures looked up in surprise.

Frederick Henzell removed the glasses which he wore for reading as his daughter came into the room. Celia looked calm and quiet as usual, but his eye, professionally experienced in summing up the mental state of a client, discerned that the calmness was a trifle forced. The set of her mouth and her straight shoulders held the suggestion of a person braced to some particular effort. The lawyer perceived at once that something disturbing to the mechanical tranquillity of his existence was about to take place.

'So she is going to be troublesome,' flashed through his mind. He frowned. It had come already, then, the moment he had half-consciously dreaded in the dining-room, the moment when some unpleasant demand would be made upon him. He felt his face settling into a mould of anticipatory opposition as it did when, in the course of his work, he had to conduct a difficult interview. At the same time he noticed with proprietary appreciation Celia's erect figure, the brilliant sheen of her hair which, since she had come home, she had 'put up' in a loose, gleaming knot. 'She's grown into a fine looking girl,' thought the father. But instead of softening his attitude this thought led on to one which increased his resentment with its hint of further domestic upheavals. 'She'll have to come out soon; and then Marion will have to be persuaded to do some entertaining for her.'

'Well, what is it, Celia?' he was saying in his polite, rather dry voice, as the girl did not at once start to speak.

'Father, could I talk to you alone for a few minutes?'

The determination with which these words were spoken was matched by the level gaze of the blue eyes, so like those of the lawyer, whose discouraging stare they now steadily encountered.

From the head of the family, in a chill, disapproving tone, came the reply:

'My dear Celia, you can't possibly have anything to say to me which should not be said in front of your mother.'

'Very well, then. It was only that I didn't want mother to be upset—'

Mrs. Henzell's expression had been growing more and more apprehensive since her daughter's entry. She now let the knitting fall on to her knee, and lifting her hands which, singularly small and wrinkled, somewhat resembled the claws of a parrot in their curving gestures, interjected a timid protest.

'My dear child, whatever it is you want to say to your father could surely wait till the morning. This is hardly the time to disturb—'

'It's the only time I have a chance to speak to him, Mother.' With a look that was impatient without being unkind, the girl stooped to return to her mother's lap the ball of grey wool that had rolled on to the floor before she once more tackled the lawyer.

'It's about my going to Oxford. I know you wrote and told Miss Rowe that we couldn't afford it, but won't you please think it over again? I promise you that I wouldn't be extravagant. I wouldn't cost you a penny more than was absolutely essential. It means so much to me, Father . . . I'd work very hard and I'm sure I could do well in the examinations. Won't you give me a chance?'

'You have heard my final decision. I do not intend to discuss the matter any further.'

These two short phrases, precisely enunciated, seemed to emerge, as if by clockwork, from the stiff mask of disapproval confronting her.

'But, Father — please! Don't you think you're being rather unfair to me? If Harold had lived he'd have gone to Oxford, wouldn't he? You'd have found the money to pay for him somehow.'

The mention of the dead boy had a curious and marked

28

effect upon the atmosphere of the room and upon its occupants. It was as if a high charge of electricity had been passed through the stagnant air, a force so potent that the position of every object was instantaneously altered by an infinitesimal degree. A peculiar flicker, like the preliminary onset of a nervous spasm, crossed the lawyer's face and his cheeks became suffused with dark blood. There was an instant of intensely painful suspense. Then from the woman in the chair came a low, tremulous moan.

'Harold . . . My poor boy! How can you speak of him so heartlessly! How can you drag his name into it!'

As if his wife's protest had broken a spell, Frederick Henzell emerged from his speechless rigidity and went to her side.

'Come, come!' he said in the tone which made people speak of him as a model husband to the querulous, ailing woman. 'Don't let yourself get agitated or you'll bring on one of your headaches.'

Then, as she made no response beyond a deep sigh, he gently assisted her to her feet and propelled her across the room.

'Let me help you upstairs. This has been too much for you. You'd better lie down and I'll tell Mattie to bring your Benger's up to your room.'

From the door he addressed his daughter in a very different tone.

'You see what comes of your insubordinate attitude. I trust that your poor mother's distress will be a lesson to you never to reopen this subject or to question my future decisions for your welfare.'

'It was you who forced me to speak in front of mother,' the girl returned listlessly, as, with eyes that had now

29

acquired their odd, unfocused detachment, she noticed the straggling wisps of fine hair on Marion Henzell's bowed neck.

Celia did not immediately leave the room after her parents' exit. Instead, she stood by the fire, drumming on the mantelpiece with absent fingers. The hands of the clock stood at eight-fifty-eight: the interview which had represented her final bid to direct her future into a chosen channel had lasted exactly six minutes. She had not really hoped for any successful result to come from that interview. But it had cost her an effort for which she had had to screw up all her determination, and, now that the effort had been made and had definitely failed, she felt flat and dispirited.

A lethargy that was partly due to depression and partly to reluctance to leave the warmth of the fire kept her standing with one foot on the low brass fender. Her eyes travelled aimlessly round the room with which she was less familiar than she was with other rooms of the house and which she saw the more critically because of her recent absence at school. A fleeting vision of the head-mistress's study at Saint Ermins passed before her. By contrast with the pleasant, orderly brightness of Miss Rowe's sanctum, the room where she was now standing seemed ugly, muddled and comfortless. And yet it was the most cheerful room in the house. What a gloomy place Desborough House was! Gloomy without the distinction of dignity. As she stood there by the subsiding fire, she was contemplating a confused mental impression of her home, a composite impression built up of too-high, cube-like rooms, of cold grey window panes at the turn of

30

the stairs, of the melancholy closing of distant doors, of dark, perfidious ivy leaves pressed like the ears of countless eavesdroppers to the walls. Simultaneously with this conception of Desborough House, there existed in her mind an obscure recognition of the necessity of escaping before she too, like her mother and father, became a prisoner of the dreary genius of the place.

The study was very still. Only the canary, disturbed by the recent voices or perhaps by Celia's unaccustomed presence, chirped once or twice restlessly, and stirred in its draped cage with mouse-like scrabblings. With startling suddenness the clock began pinging the hour. *Ping-ping-ping-ping-ping-ping-ping-ping-ping*, went its hurried, staccato strokes, shrill and insistent as the yapping of a Pomeranian dog. Jerked out of her inertia by the sound, the girl moved away, out into the dimly-lit hall. For a second she had the impression that there was someone else there, that another figure was moving opposite her in the shadows. When she realized that it was her own reflexion in the mirror of the hat-stand which moved, she went across and stood in front of the glass. Over the handles of sticks and umbrellas she gazed at herself in the ghostly luminous square. Her face stared back at her mysteriously, pale, young, enigmatic, under the bright hair; the face of a naiad submerged. It gave her a sense of deep satisfaction to look at that face. The pleasure which she derived from looking at her own reflexion was something impossible to describe, quiet and almost solemn.

THE fear-ridden soul of Marion Henzell dreaded the
winter; but the summer also held its own terrors for her
with its trying heat and thundery days that were almost
certain to bring on a headache. Now it was past the middle
of September and the summer was over. The jobbing
gardener who came three times a week to keep the grounds
tidy had said that there had been a touch of frost that
morning.

As she slowly ascended the stairs for her afternoon rest,
Mrs. Henzell thought apprehensively about the coming
winter which appeared to her like a long, bleak, treacherous corridor, full of draughts and sly aches and pains,
down which she must painfully tread. She had a special
reason for dreading this particular winter: a reason connected with her daughter Celia whose eighteenth birthday would fall in a few days time.

The girl had been at home all the summer and had
given no trouble to anyone. True, she was not very help-
ful in the house and she disliked prising dandelions and
plantains out of the lawn, the weedlessness of which the
solicitor was so proud. But after that one unfortunate outburst just after her return from school she had made no
more trouble, apparently settling down, amenably if
rather silently, to the life of Desborough House; occupying all her spare time with scribbling or with long walks
in the country. It was not Celia's own behaviour that
caused her mother so much anxiety, but the ultimatum
which Frederick Henzell had delivered about his daughter.

As far back as the early spring the lawyer had broached

the subject of some entertaining at Desborough House on Celia's account. They really must give one or two parties for the girl, let her get out and meet a few people, he had said. Mrs. Henzell had listened with growing horror as it became apparent to her that his suggestion would force her back into the world she had renounced completely since her son's death. The idea filled the soul-sick woman with consternation. She *could* not do it, even to please Frederick. Social contacts now appeared to her not only almost impossible to achieve but supernaturally terrifying. She could not have been more alarmed if she had been asked to throw open her home to a race of demons. It seemed to her that she would rather die than emerge from her seclusion.

So she had begun to make excuses. The girl was too young, only just out of the schoolroom; it would be better to wait a little. Then, with the coming of summer, she had made her own health a pretext for procrastination. She was fit for nothing in the hot weather and, anyhow, everybody went away from Jessington in July and August. 'Very well,' the lawyer had said in the cut-and-dried voice which implied that he had spoken his last word on the subject and would brook no argument or appeal: 'She shall come out at the beginning of the autumn when she is eighteen.'

Throughout the summer Marion Henzell had been haunted by the spectre of the ordeal before her, while all sorts of fantasies had flourished secretly in her warped brain. Perhaps, after all, Frederick would relent and let Celia go to Oxford. Perhaps she would herself be stricken with a form of illness that would make social activities impossible. Perhaps she might even die. Perhaps something would happen to Celia. The girl might run away. Or, at one of the few more or less public functions to which she went with her father, she might take the fancy of a wealthy woman who would offer to chaperone her.

Now, when none of these things had occurred and Celia's birthday was drawing inexorably nearer, the mother felt almost distracted. Any day now her husband might begin to talk about invitations and dates. 'How can I face it?' she whispered plaintively as she entered her bedroom. She really wished herself dead.

Her sense of injury was augmented by the fact that the room felt chilly. Both the windows were open and a keen autumnal air was alternately sucking and billowing the double curtains. Mrs. Henzell went to close one of the windows. That was the worst of Mattie; she never realized when the temperature changed. Just because the windows had been left open all the summer they were left open now. She pushed down the sash but raised it immediately to free a leaf that had been caught underneath. The ivy from Harold's grave had climbed right over this wall of the house and framed the window sill with a dado of dark leaves. The bitter scent of the crushed ivy leaf came to her nostrils as she carefully lowered the sash again. Her pale eyes flickered suddenly as she caught sight of someone moving outside. It certainly seemed to her that she had caught a glimpse of Celia's blue skirt disappearing near some bushes at the bottom of the garden. What was the girl doing? It was not nearly warm enough to sit out of doors and she could not be going for a walk as there was no way out of the garden in that direction.

The anxious-faced woman stood watching for a moment to see if her child reappeared. Then she turned away and began her preparations for lying down on the bed. 'Perhaps she's gone to do some weeding on the lower lawn by the river,' she told herself. But she did not really believe this. A distant qualm, an instantly-silenced whisper of guilt assailed her. What did she know of her daughter's activities? What lay behind all these solitary walks, this eternal scribbling in exercise books? Sighing, she pulled the heavy eiderdown over her feet and buried her face in the pillow. She had quite enough to worry her as it was. Why invite further troubles when the easiest course was to take it for granted that other people were all right?

Quite unconscious of having been seen from the window, Celia hurried through the sloping garden. Her face, if either of her parents had been there to see it, would have surprised them with its glow of vitality. Her mind was busy with secret thoughts. How lucky it was that her mother always rested, leaving her with the whole afternoon to do as she pleased. At the foot of the garden a fairly steep bank, topped with a privet hedge, sloped down to the river Jess. At one point the line of the hedge was broken by a flight of stone steps leading to the water. An observant person might have noticed that the moss which for years had covered these steps had, towards the middle, latterly been worn away.

The girl went down the steps and looked over the water, low now at the end of summer. 'Clare!' she called guardedly. The bushes beside her bent in the wind, emitting a melancholy sighing sound that complemented the unconscious pathos of the young voice drifting over the vacant stream. From behind a projecting clump of willows on her left there appeared a young man paddling a boat into which she stepped quickly. The two hardly spoke until they were out of sight of the garden of Desborough House. A sharp wind caught them at the bend of the stream.

'Not much chance of being noticed to-day! Nobody's likely to be on the river now it's turned so cold. Let's make for our backwater — we'll be sheltered there.' Celia picked up a paddle while she was speaking, and as a result of their combined efforts the clumsy boat drove through the water.

VII

CLARE BRYANT was twenty-four years old but younger, except in the matter of actual years, than his companion. His pleasant, warm-coloured, typically Anglo-Saxon face with its faint fair fluff of down, could sometimes look positively infantile in spite of the well-set-up masculine form it surmounted. Just now, as his torso moved rhythmically with the effortless, muscular swing of his arms, he looked the perfect example of the healthy young Aryan male. He looked good-tempered, dependable and not too intelligent: the sort of young man who would do excellently in an official post of minor responsibility — just such a position, in fact, as he did hold. Later on, perhaps, he would develop more outstanding characteristics, though the somewhat ineffectual droop of his lips made this seem improbable, as did also the sentimental, unpractical, student-type of romanticism that gave his eyes such a soft beam.

'I wish the summer hadn't gone so fast,' he was saying: and it seemed incredible that the months of July, August and September had once stretched before him like so many years of boredom.

Clare was an orphan and had been brought up by an aunt who, not at all fond of children, had been grimly determined to do her best for the boy. She was not well off, and he had been sent to a sound though undistinguished grammar school for his education. This over, he had graduated, via the training shops, to an engineering job in the East where he had already spent three years. During this period abroad his aunt had died. The young man had not been anxious to go on leave. So normal in every other respect, in this one thing he felt himself different from his fellows, that the thought of an English holiday did not attract him. If possible, he would have postponed his leave, but it was a rule of the company that young employees should return home after three years on health grounds.

Back in England, he did not know what to do with himself. He had no family ties. He had no money besides his pay, for his aunt had only possessed a small annuity which had ceased at her death. He could not afford to stop in London having what is called 'a good time'. After he had done a little mild celebrating and had visited a few old school-friends, the summer months still lay interminably ahead of him. He had already booked his return passage on the earliest possible boat, but the three months still had to be got through somehow. It was at this point that a distant relative, a cousin of his aunt's whom he could scarcely remember, wrote inviting him to visit her.

The invitation had been issued purely out of kind-heartedness and accepted merely from boredom. But once the visitor was installed in the Jessington home of Mrs. Marriott and her husband his stay prolonged itself indefinitely. Clare was one of those well-mannered, naturally considerate young men who always have a great deal of success with elderly people and especially with elderly women. He soon stood very high in Mrs. Marriott's good graces. He was quiet and yet entertaining; considerate and charming: he had only to behave in his natural way and he could not help winning her favour. It certainly cost him no effort to be amiable to the kindly old woman for whom he quickly felt a sincere regard. She, for her part, was delighted with her guest. The presentable, polite, boyish Clare was a great asset in the drawing-rooms of middle-aged Jessington society. She took him everywhere with her, and it was at a garden party given by the mayor and mayoress that he was introduced to Celia Henzell.

Somehow — in the improbable way that friendships between young people do ripen in spite of all obstacles — somehow the two became better acquainted. They met again a few times at the more formal social functions which Celia attended with her father. Then they began to meet secretly, to go for long walks together in the adjacent country, to idle away warm afternoons in a boat on the Jess. The sluggish river was a godsend to them, passing, as it did, both their gardens, and affording a simple and not easily suspected meeting-place and mode of escape.

Clare Bryant had been strongly attracted by Celia from the first. His innate romanticism was stirred as much by the curious seclusion in which she lived as by her unusual appearance. With her reddish-gold hair and her pale enigmatic face, she seemed to him like the traditional fairy princess locked in a secret tower. She was quite different from the other Jessington girls to whom he had been introduced. These wholesome, red-cheeked misses with their attendant match-making mammas, appeared like frolicsome cart-horses by contrast with Celia's poised, fine-drawn grace. She had confided to him that she was writing a book, and this, too, gave her a glamour. His life so far had not included close friendship with a person of the opposite sex. It was a new and enchanting experience for him. He now wished very much that he had not got to leave England so soon.

The boat had reached the backwater, and by unspoken

39

consent its occupants ceased paddling, allowing themselves to drift into the shelter of the high bank topped by a dying forest of thistle and willow-herb. This quiet river-world had fallen under the spell of autumn and its sleepy air held the perfume of decay. Sunlight filtered thinly through the overhanging vegetation. The wandering sun rays touched hundreds of delicate floating seeds and filaments sailing through the air like tiny vessels of tender light. The stillness under the bank seemed unreal, while in the real world above wind was teasing the branches of bushes where yellow leaves showed bright among the green.

The young people took little notice of all this, yet the indescribable sense of things drawing towards an end had its effect on them, plunging them into a wistful mood.

'Only a bit more than a week and then I'll have to be off,' said the man.

'But your boat doesn't sail for over a fortnight.'

'I shall have to spend at least a few days in Town, getting my kit together and so on.'

The girl gave him one of her queerly un-girlish looks, speculative and aware. He did not notice. He was edging the boat slowly along, catching at the strong stems of fading weeds on the bank.

'You talk as if you didn't want to go, Clare,' she said in a moment. 'And yet I thought you were so looking forward to going back to the East.'

A stem broke off in his hand and he threw it into the water and watched it float away before he replied.

'I am looking forward to it — at least, I was, until just lately. Now everything seems different.'

Once more her glance rested upon him, so much less innocent than her pleasant voice.

'Why is that, do you think?'

It was very still under the bank. Only small twitterings and rustlings of birds and the muffled bark of a far distant dog came like sounds from another world.

'It's because of you!' he burst out impulsively. 'Everything's changed since I got to know you, Celia. Nothing else seems important any more —'

With satisfaction she watched the melting gleam of warm, almost Teutonic sentimentality well up like boyish tears in his eyes.

VIII

ON the night before her daughter's marriage Mrs. Henzel slept badly. She had spent most of the preceding day resting upon her bed, and perhaps that was why, when night came, she felt restless and unable to settle down. 'You must save yourself to-day,' Mattie had told her when she brought up her morning tea. 'We can't have you feeling tired or headachy to-morrow.' The faithful old servant had found time amidst all her other extra work to hurry upstairs every hour or so to attend to her mistress, carrying up countless trays of weak tea and toast. 'How you spoil me, Mattie!' Mrs. Henzell had said. 'One might almost think that I was the bride!' And indeed a stranger entering Desborough House would have found the mother rather than the daughter the centre of interest and attention.

At bedtime Frederick Henzell had come into his wife's room. Standing beside the double bed which he had not shared for over a decade, the lawyer's straight, spare, angular form had loomed like a post above the woman lying on the pillows with a thin, grey plait of hair one over shoulder. It had given her a shock to see him there. His unaccustomed presence had brought home to her for the first time the reality of what was about to happen. For days she had lived in a flutter of excitement, but never until now had the actual realization of what it was all about penetrated her self-absorption. Her husband spoke with his usual mechanical consideration, advising her to take one of the tablets which the doctor had prescribed for her periodic fits of insomnia. 'It's most important that you should have a good night and feel fresh to-morrow,' he told her; and he had found the round, black pill-box and left it on the table within easy teach of her hand.

When he had retired into his room and left her alone she swallowed the tablet. A confused fear of 'drugs' made her dislike taking a hypnotic, even under doctor's orders; but on this occasion she did not hesitate to gulp down the innocuous looking pellet. This was an emergency. The quite pleasant sense of importance which for the last few days had wrapped her round like cotton-wool had suddenly been stripped away. For some reason or other her husband's appearance in the bedroom had shocked her out of her fantasy world and forced her to contemplate reality. The contemplation was highly disturbing: she would escape it by going to sleep.

She slept uneasily for two hours and then woke with a start from an alarming dream. Her mouth was dry, her heart beat painfully in her thin breast, she had a feeling of suffocation that did not leave her for several moments. She sat up in bed, trembling and gasping for breath. Presently the disagreeable physical symptoms subsided and she began to feel calmer, more normal. But now there supervened a mental inquietude that was just as distressing.

It was a bright night outside, and in spite of the thick curtains the room was not totally dark. Her eyes dimly discerned the shapes of furniture; her nostrils inhaled the faint, well-known odour of medicines and lavender water; her ears caught through the open door of the adjoining room the solicitor's steady breathing. All these familiar things were powerless to reassure her.

In the silent solitude of the night her anxiety mounted. She knew what had awakened her: it was the pang of a guilty conscience that had penetrated even the numbing effect of the sleeping draught and called her to confront her own soul. To-morrow her daughter was to be married. Or perhaps it was morning already, perhaps the day had already dawned when she was to part with her child to a stranger.

What did she know of this Clare Bryant? Nothing, except that he was to take her daughter thousands of miles away to a strange continent. A vaguely terrifying picture floated before her, a vision of jungles where snakes writhed in the undergrowth and huge beasts lurked with evil, predatory eyes. She had condemned her daughter to this: and why? In order to achieve her own cowardly and selfish ends.

All through the summer she had prayed that something might happen to deliver her from the responsibility she dreaded, to spare her the awful effort of making a return to the world. And like a miracle, at the very last moment, something had happened. Celia had announced her intention of marrying Clare. To Marion Henzell it had come like a reprieve from death. There would be no need, after all, for her to sacrifice her precious seclusion. The young man was leaving the country at once; there would be no time for ceremony or social affairs, no time for anything except the very simplest of weddings. Just the one public appearance to make and then she could return, and for ever this time, to her private world of memories and the small sensual pleasures of food and warmth which sufficed for her content.

She had exerted herself, more than she had done for years, to achieve this unexpected salvation. With a cunning she did not know she possessed, she had employed arguments and let fall subtle suggestions to overcome her

44

husband's first instinctive opposition, until, artfully, she had succeeded in making him think that he had arranged the match. She had visited shops. She had talked to strange people.

In her agitation it now appeared to her that by her will she had brought the marriage about. She had more than half known of Celia's secret assignations; if she had wished she could have nipped the affair in the bud. But she had not wished. It was to her advantage that the affair should continue. She had sacrificed her daughter's happiness and future to her own ends. It never occurred to her that the marriage might turn out happily or that the young people might be really fond of one another.

A goods train shunting on the line half a mile away had all this time formed a background to her thoughts with its monotonous diminuendo of muffled crashes. These sounds, for so many years the accompaniment to her nocturnal meditations that she was hardly aware of them, now ceased, and the resulting stillness seemed to acquire a new and sinister quality. The clock of a near-by church — the church where Celia's wedding was to take place — struck two with that peculiar effect of portentous solemnity which clocks acquire in the silent hours of the night. The wind-borne strokes seemed to the listening woman to be charged with stern significance. The fatal day had already arrived. In a panic she threw back her coverings and climbed out of bed, wrapping herself automatically in her thick Jaeger dressing-gown. Her feet seemed to find their own way into the woollen slippers and to carry her of their own accord across the unlighted room.

FREDERICK HENZELL was sleeping the sleep of the just. When earlier that evening he had entered his wife's room and had stood by her bedside, he too had experienced rather a queer sensation. What was it, what obscure atmospheric magic had suddenly revealed Marion to him in the clear light of objectivity? Even while he heard his own voice speaking customary soothing words in its customary calm tone, a small part of his consciousness had been standing apart, looking with a novel attention at the familiar reclining female shape. That small part of his consciousness observed with surprise that Marion Henzell was an old woman.

When he had withdrawn to his own room the lawyer looked long and carefully at his reflexion in the mirror between the two gas-brackets, both of which he had lighted, contrary to his usual economical procedure.

If Marion were an old woman, it followed that he, her senior by several years, must be an old man. Gazing back at him from the glass he saw a rather severe, closed-looking face with a small grey moustache and an aspect of hale alertness. No one could possibly say that there was anything senile in his appearance. But all the same, it was impossible to evade the fact that he was no longer young.

As he undressed for the night, carefully folding each garment and putting each toilet article in its appointed place, an unprecedented thought-sequence was passing through his head. The greater portion of his life had passed, and he had not noticed its passing. There had been a young man called Frederick Henzell who had unobtrusively vanished, and in his place there had appeared mysteriously an old man bearing the same name. What had become of the young Frederick Henzell and his thoughts and ambitions? And what had happened to the boy called Harold who had once run about the house with an eager face? Had he vanished utterly, or did he exist somewhere in the immensity of the moon-lit night — were he and young Frederick perhaps together somewhere?

The solicitor took his toothbrush out of the china receptacle and started to brush his teeth vigorously, first sideways and then up and down in the way he believed to be most effective, as if at the same time to brush away his unorthodox thoughts. The measure was successful, for by the time he had rinsed, dried and replaced the brush he felt much more his usual self. He was a man of responsible position whose son had died many years ago and whose wife was an invalid. Both of these latter circumstances were unfortunate but by no means uncommon or especially tragic. They in no way minimized the successful achievements of his professional life.

And to-morrow his daughter was to be married to a young man of good prospects, pleasing qualities and apparently blameless character. This thought, at any rate, contained no suggestion of anything that was not absolutely normal and propitious. As Frederick Henzell lighted his bedside candle and turned out the gas, he remembered the time, only a few months back, when Celia had caused him some uneasiness. All that nonsense about going to Oxford and taking a degree and costing him goodness knows how much during the process — young Bryant had put that out of her head quickly enough!

How well everything had turned out after all, he

reflected as he got into bed. He felt as pleased as if he had brought off a clever stroke of business — almost as pleased as if he had sold Desborough House! And certainly it was a gratifying transaction, settling the girl happily for life and getting her off his hands at the same time. Marion, too, had behaved remarkably well. It would have been natural enough if she had opposed the marriage and made endless scenes. But instead of that she had taken it all quite sensibly.

Yes, everything had turned out well; so well that he had felt he could afford to be generous and to settle a little money on his daughter. Clare's salary was, of course, small as yet, and that extra hundred a year would make all the difference to the young people's *ménage*. To do the boy justice, he certainly had not tried to sponge on his future father-in-law. He had actually seemed quite reluctant to agree to the settlement, saying that he thought a husband ought to be able to provide for his wife himself. Nobody could accuse him of being mercenary. The fact that the young man would have been willing to marry Celia without any dowry made her father feel that he himself had acted with real benevolence, although the sum in question was not exactly princely. He might so easily have given the girl nothing at all, and instead he had insisted on behaving generously. A warm feeling of complacency counteracted the chill of the sheets as he blew out the candle and lay down to sleep the sleep not only of the just but of the munificent.

It seemed to him that he had only slept for a few minutes when Marion woke him. Familiar with his wife's nervous peculiarities, he knew at once what was happening and reached for the matches in the first instant of waking. It was in anticipation of some such nocturnal alarm

48

that the door between their two rooms was always left open.

'What is the matter?' he asked at once. His voice sounded quite normal, but he could not really have been perfectly awake, for, just for a second, before the candle was fully alight and while great shadows were reeling about the walls, the small figure beside him with its plaited hair seemed like that of a schoolgirl.

A brief amazement flashed through the lawyer's mind at the tricks his senses were playing upon him to-night, first revealing the familiar partner of his life as an old woman and then, shortly afterwards, as a mere child. No doubt he was over-tired and slightly out-of-sorts; the last few days had been trying, although he had not been conscious of any great strain.

'What is the matter, Marion?' he repeated. 'Are you unwell?'

An odd, smothered sound broke from her, and his eyes, growing used to the wavering light, saw that there were tears on her cheeks.

'This wedding, Frederick!' she gasped. 'We must stop it!'

Wide awake now, feeling quite his rational, unemotional self, and managing, even in his pyjamas, to look dignified and somewhat forbidding, the lawyer sat up in bed.

'Don't be hysterical, Marion,' he said in a severe tone. 'Pull yourself together and stop talking wildly. Of course the wedding will take place as we have arranged.'

'Celia's so young . . . Just a child.'

'Eighteen is a very good age for a girl to marry. My mother married at eighteen. There is a tendency nowadays for young people to postpone marriage far too long.'

'But how can she know . . .? She doesn't understand what she's doing.'

Frederick Henzell compressed his lips to a thin line under his tidy moustache. He had been working particularly hard of late, and then this business of the marriage on top of everything, all arrangements having to be made in such indecorous haste, had really been very exhausting. He really needed his nights' sleep. And here was Marion, so inconsiderately disturbing his rest and making a scene at this hour; working herself up for one of her headaches, most likely.

'You must go back to bed. You'll get cold standing there,' he said. And then, as a distant misgiving pierced him, he added: 'What do you mean when you say that she doesn't know what she's doing? I presume that you have acquainted her with the facts of life?'

His wife's only response was to burst into renewed tears and to cover her face with her hands.

Perceiving that he would have to employ other tactics if he wished to be left in peace, the solicitor stretched up and patted her arm which felt brittle and thin as a stick under the woolly sleeve.

'There! There! Don't distress yourself. I'm sure you've always done your duty as a mother,' he was saying, while at the same time he thought to himself: 'I suppose women often have these emotional storms just before their daughters are married.'

'You're tired now and overwrought,' he went on in a voice which contrived to blend the necessary note of sympathy with a bracing matter-of-factness. 'Things often seem distorted at night. In the morning you'll feel quite differently about it all. Now get back to bed, my dear, and try to go to sleep again.'

To his immense relief he perceived that she was going to obey. She uncovered her face, wiped her eyes and tightened the cord of her dressing-gown. The noise of the shunting trains had started again outside in the dark.

'Take this candle with you,' he said considerately, concealing a yawn. 'Otherwise you may trip over something.'

On the night before her wedding Celia sat up in bed until twelve o'clock going through the exercise books which contained the manuscript of her unfinished novel. She read the pages of neat handwriting with as much detachment as possible. Finally she decided that the work, though not as good as she had hoped, was not at all bad. She realized that she would not be able to do any writing for some time to come. Nevertheless, she was determined not to lose the continuity, the sense of intimate contact with her characters. She would keep the manuscript handy, on the top of her trunk where she could easily get at it whenever she had the opportunity of a quiet half-hour. Later on, when they were established in their Eastern home, she would have as much time for it as she wanted, while Clare was away at his work.

She did not at once put out the light when she had finished reading. She was not at all sleepy, but felt full of the quiet kind of excitement which she had been accustomed to feel before an examination; an un-urgent, low-level kind of excitement that was quite pleasurable.

She looked at the room which was not the old nursery but one of the smaller bedrooms into which she had moved when she first started to go to school. It had been re-papered then in a white wallpaper with shiny perpendicular stripes that accentuated the height of the ceiling. It was a badly proportioned room, far too high for its size, like the inside of a tall white box. This room and the cold little ante-room downstairs had been the setting for most of her life at Desborough House. Now the bedroom, denuded of her belongings, looked exceedingly bare and chilly — more than ever like an empty white box. Her modest luggage, the trunk she had taken to school, a big old-fashioned leather suitcase, a handbag, a hat-box and a steamer rug in a strap, lay neatly piled by the dressing-table.

Celia did not feel the slightest regret at the prospect of leaving her home. She had made up her mind long ago to leave it at the first opportunity, and now she was merely carrying out her resolve. Neither did she feel the slightest regret at the prospect of parting from her parents. Her father and mother, though they had treated her with adequate kindness, had never either displayed or demanded affection. Any such display would, in fact, have been as embarrassing to them as to her. Without any special resentment she knew that she was unimportant: both to her father centred in his professional interests, and to her mother isolated in the unreal world of the neurasthenic. Both of them would secretly be glad to be rid of her disturbing presence. She did not exactly define these facts in her mind; she merely sensed and accepted them with the casualness of long familiarity.

Something made her tilt her head back and look up to where a photograph of a young man with sentimental eyes hung on the wall over her bed. The words written in ink across the bottom of the picture appeared distorted from her angle of vision, but she could just make them out: 'Celia, with all my love.' She had forgotten to pack the photograph of her fiancé. Because it was hanging immediately over her head, she had overlooked it just now in her survey of the room.

A sort of blank came in her mind when she thought of Clare Bryant. In spite of the photograph, she could not even remember clearly what he looked like. To-morrow they were going to be married and she ought to be thinking about him. But she lay blankly in bed and stared at the empty room. What was Clare doing now? Probably he was sound asleep, dreaming, quite likely, about the day in the boat when they became engaged. Recalling the soft, spaniel look in his eyes, she smiled faintly. 'Just like a German student . . . can one get really fond of a person like that?' But she remembered his simple, undemanding, straightforward friendliness, and there was some warmth in her smile. She did not love him in the least. But there was a grateful response to his friendship somewhere within her. 'Am I wronging him?' she wondered. 'But he fell in love with me of his own accord. And I expect I'll make him as good a wife as anyone else would.' It was wonderfully fortunate for her that anyone as likeable as Clare had appeared so opportunely to save her from Desborough House.

She put out the light and at once fell asleep. But her sleep was light and through it she could hear all the time the noise of the shunting trucks on the railway line. The distant crashes appeared in her dream like beads on a string. Sometimes the string broke and the beads exploded violently into darkness. She thought in the dream that this was what life was: one bead following another upon a string until the string snapped, and then . . . what? She seemed to be both awake and asleep as she lay there in bed, hearing sounds now in the house itself.

The boards of the landing creaked. Someone was evidently coming towards her room. The door handle turned hesitantly with its slight grating noise, the hinges emitted a whine. 'It's mother; and I don't want to talk to her. I want to go on sleeping,' Celia thought. She had

54

an instinctive dread of becoming involved in some pseudo-intimate conversation which would seem shocking and even obscene between two such disconnected individuals.

'Celia!' Marion Henzell whispered from the doorway.

'Yes, Mother? What do you want? Is anything wrong?'

There was a pause. Celia could hear an engine with a heavy load puffing wheezily in the distance. Then the elder woman came right into the room and shut the door. In the moonlight from the uncurtained window the daughter could see rather clearly her lined, querulous face. A sensation of fastidious withdrawal passed through her heart.

'Celia . . . about this marriage . . . I'm so worried . . . Are you quite sure . . .? I mean to say, it's your whole life that's in question . . . Don't let anybody influence you — '

The girl sat up.

'Mother, what are you talking about? Of course I'm quite sure I want to marry Clare.'

Marion Henzell was clasping and unclasping her hands.

'But do you understand . . . Are you sure you know what marriage means? It's a mother's duty to explain these things to her daughter . . . ', there was a sound of tears in her voice, 'and I've not told you anything.'

Celia was struck by the note of misery underlying the words. Her mother's voice had seemed to betray all the sense of lonely inadequacy that had accumulated in her unbalanced brain during interminable melancholy days and nights. When Celia saw the nervously twitching hands she felt a faint current of sympathy run over her own nerves. 'How unhappy she must have been all these years!'

'Don't worry about that, Mother,' she said. 'A girl at

55

school told me about having babies, if that's what you mean. Her father was a doctor, and she read it all up in medical books.'

She had purposely made her voice sound casual, and now she could have laughed at the blend of horror and relief that appeared on her mother's countenance.

'Oh, well, of course . . . in that case . . .' Mrs. Henzell drew a deep breath like a sigh, picked up a corner of the bedspread and after fingering it for a few moments let it fall back in its place. She clearly wished to say something more, to establish a closer contact between them. But, receiving no encouragement from her daughter, she wished her good-night, pecked her uncertainly on the cheek with her thin lips, and went out of the room.

Celia stared absent-mindedly at the place where she had been standing, then lay down suddenly and pulled the bedclothes round her shoulders with a decisive movement.

'How do you feel now, Mrs. Bryant?'

The nurse, hastily summoned from the big town in the plains to attend young Mrs. Bryant's confinement, had arrived some little time ago and, finding her patient quietly resting, had merely asked her a few questions and had then retired to wash and change and recover after her exhausting railway journey. Now she opened the door of Celia's bedroom again.

'I feel just the same, I think.'

'The pains aren't coming any more often?'

'No, I don't think so.'

In her thin lilac wrapper, faded from many rough washings and slappings on river stones, Celia sat up laboriously and contemplated the woman who was to be her companion in the shattering experience of birth. The nurse was much younger than she had expected; probably not more than three or four years older than her patient. The neat blue and white uniform gave her a semblance of efficiency, but her pallid, heavy-eyed face did not inspire much confidence.

'You look tired,' Celia said. 'Wouldn't you like to rest a bit longer? I shall be all right for the present.' For some reason she wanted to keep the other woman out of the room as long as possible.

'I don't need any more rest, thanks. I'm not tired, really. It was just the journey that was trying.'

'It must have been terribly hot in the train.'

'It was rather ghastly. And the heat down in the plains has been awful. Much worse than it is here.'

'Well, it won't be long before the cold weather now.'

'No.' The stranger hovered uncertainly, her hand on the door, unable, it seemed, to get herself out of the room. 'Well, if you're sure you're all right ... I've got one or two things to prepare — ' At last she seemed to be going.

'Yes. Of course you'll ask for anything you want? I've told Mahomet and the ayah to take their orders from you. My husband won't be back much before dinner time.'

When the door finally closed Celia continued to sit up on the bed in the same uncomfortable position. How queer it was that this unknown young woman with whom she had just been exchanging polite commonplaces would presently be a witness to her own agony. She felt strung-up and unnatural, but she was not exactly afraid of the ordeal before her. Having had no experience of pain she could not imagine it. Of course, it must be terrible; everyone said so. Yet she could not really imagine anything terrible happening to her. At all events, it was a great relief to have come to the end of this long, hateful period of discomfort and bodily distortion. Although she had felt quite well, the latter months of pregnancy had been like a penance to her, and she regarded them as so many months wasted, a stupid interruption of her life. Soon she would return to her normal self and be able to live again. 'What a clumsy, ugly process it is!' she thought for the hundredth time. 'What a fool I was to let myself get caught up in it!' She was deeply resentful of what seemed to her the insult to her young body.

It was about five o'clock. Although the hottest time of the day had passed, the wooden, four-roomed bungalow was still filled like an oven with heat. The air seemed to simmer. Through the closed shutters filtered the smoky-

58

gold light of the approaching sunset. October was a bad month. These stifling, thundery days at the end of the hot weather were enough to drive one mad. 'I've been out here nearly a whole year already,' Celia thought. She felt very discontented, as if she had been defrauded of most of the year.

The door was opening again. The nurse had returned. During her absence shadows had gathered in the corners of the shuttered bedroom, and now her white face seemed to merge with her cap into a hovering blur that had an irritating effect on her patient.

'A lady has called — a Mrs. Hailes. I don't know if you feel up to seeing her?'

'Yes, of course. Please ask her to sit down and say I'll be there in a minute.'

Celia attempted to swing herself off the bed and was annoyed because her swollen body refused to respond readily to the commands of her brain. She had never grown accustomed to the limitations of her condition. She could never remember that now she must move cautiously and slowly as if balancing a weight before her.

As she struggled into her dress she felt angry, rebellious and humiliated. She hated the shapeless dress, she hated her own face that stared back at her dimly from the mirror with a stupid, sullen expression. 'Just like an animal,' she muttered. A spasm of pain took her, but it was no worse than the pains which she had been experiencing at intervals all day; no worse than a bad menstrual pain: it was gone in a few moments. She picked up the comb that felt hot in her hand. Even her hair seemed to have lost its colour and gloss, she thought, and to have acquired a straw-like dullness.

Near the ceiling of the sitting-room a punkha was

wearily swinging, churning the stagnant air. The room was undistinguished and bare, the room of a poorly-paid subordinate official, as far as possible removed from the popular conception of Eastern luxury. Among the shabby wicker furniture a black bowl full of deep blue lilies struck a single note of beauty, piercing and pure as a bell.

From a chair near these flowers rose a rather ethereal-looking woman, at least ten years older than Celia, with a singularly spiritual face.

'So you're still up! I just called to see how you were and to lend you a few nightgowns . . .' She indicated a parcel on the bamboo table, 'One can't have too many. I thought you might be glad of them.'

'How kind of you, Winifred! You're always so kind. I don't know how I should ever have been able to face all this without you.'

Winifred Hailes was struck by the tension in her expression.

'Nonsense! You're much braver than I am,' she said, thinking that Celia was nervous and needed reassurance. 'How do you like your nurse?' she went on.

'Oh, she's all right . . ..She looks like a white mouse . . . I wish I could have gone to the hospital, though, instead of having the child here. It seems so public, somehow — almost indecent.'

The response to these words reached her only in the form of a consolatory murmur. Her attention had broken off sharply and directed itself towards the door of her bedroom where she could hear someone moving about. The nurse must have gone in there. Something clinked inside the room. The girl stood listening intently. The parcel of nightdresses, the mysterious preparations going

60

on behind the shut door, the nurse's steps tapping to and fro, all suddenly seemed strangely frightening. Even the sympathetic look on her friend's face struck her as ominous. 'Something terrible really is going to happen to me . . . quite soon . . . and there's no escape —'

Mrs. Hailes was watching her. There was an almost saint-like suggestion about her compassionate mouth, her smooth, tropical pallor. Celia suddenly felt a sharp pain, her hands clenched and jerked involuntarily. Her companion noticed the movement.

'I must be going,' she said gently. 'If I were you I should lie down again now.'

'Oh, don't go yet!'

The exclamation was as involuntary as the recent movement had been. It seemed to have been snatched from Celia unawares. The thought of being left alone in the bungalow with the nurse and her sinister preparations all at once seemed intolerable. The presence of her friend alone stood like a last frail defence between herself and the unknown terrors ahead. Her instinct was to cling to her desperately. Next moment she felt ashamed of her own lack of restraint. A painful flush overspread her face.

'I'll come as far as the gate with you,' she said, in an exaggeratedly phlegmatic tone.

The other glanced at her questioningly. Celia's flushed cheeks and abnormal manner clearly indicated an intense repressed agitation.

'Very well . . . If you're sure you ought to be walking about,' she said, humouring her.

They went outside together. A few wooden steps led down from the door to the parched compound. Near the foot of the steps, the *mali*, naked except for a loincloth, crouched over some sickly plants and observed the Englishwomen with black, darting eyes from beyond the impassable barrier of his race. A bank of enormous, lava-coloured clouds had covered the setting sun. The atmosphere, stale and vitiated after the heat of the day, felt heavier than air; more like some tepid, heavy gas intolerably charged with the force of the storm which would not break. A group of tall trees near the gate held aloft their motionless, sparse foliage that belonged to no special season. These trees seemed unnaturally large, flat and colourless, as if carved out of lead. The sky appeared almost to rest on their top branches. A vast, unseen insect life filled the world with its high-pitched buzzing. In the livid light under the huge trees the two women looked small and quenched, Celia moving awkwardly with a swaying gait.

'How I wish I hadn't got to go through with this business!' she broke out suddenly. A feverish desire to talk was upon her. She felt a craving to express herself, to pour out all the secret emotions that were usually locked firmly within her. 'You'll think I'm a coward . . . and I suppose I am. Yet if it were for the sake of something I really wanted, I honestly believe I could endure anything. But I don't want this child — I never have wanted it. Clare does . . . but I don't . . . Yet I'm the one who has to suffer. It all seems so senseless!'

'Strange girl!' thought Winifred Hailes. This way of talking was very unacceptable to her. 'But she doesn't mean what she's saying. She's thoroughly overwrought. Yet she always seems so cold and restrained. Who would have thought she had such violent feelings?'

'Do I shock you talking like this, Winifred? I couldn't say these things to anyone but you. I wouldn't say them now if I didn't feel so frightened. I feel very frightened and depressed — and there's no one I can talk to. I've never been able to communicate with people.'

A voice from the bungalow interrupted this outburst. The nurse had come to the top of the steps and was watching them.

'Don't overtire yourself, Mrs. Bryant,' she called out disapprovingly. 'I think perhaps you should come inside now.'

Mrs. Hailes took Celia's hand and pressed it between her own. The girl's fingers felt dry and burning.

'Good-bye till to-morrow,' she said in a low voice. 'And good luck. Don't worry about things. I understand how you feel now. But as soon as the baby's there you'll find that you love it very much.'

She would have liked to kiss her friend, but something in her attitude made this impossible. Celia's unnatural excitement had vanished as quickly as it had come. It was impossible to think of embracing that heavy, obstinate looking figure. The adjective 'wooden' came into her mind, but in the weird volcanic light it was really some ashen effigy of motherhood that Celia resembled.

XII

Nurse Ward was not at all pleased when she found that
it was her turn to take on the Bryant case. 'Isn't it just
my luck?' she complained to her friends at the hospital.
The nurses took private patients in strict rotation, there
was no possibility of favouritism or unfairness. Yet it
seemed to Josephine Ward that those cases which fell to
her share were always the most 'remote and the least
desirable.

She had been working in the East for eighteen months
now; long enough for the novelty and excitement to have
worn off, but not long enough for her to start thinking
about leave. The hot weather had been a severe trial to
her; never a very robust girl, she now felt absolutely
limp and exhausted — 'Just a chewed rag,' as she said
to herself. It was really deadly, all this hard work in the
appalling tropical heat. If only she could have had a
few days' rest she could have carried on all right. But
instead of that, here she was, sent off to attend this
wretched Bryant woman at the back of beyond.

Still grumbling inwardly, she sat in the slow, suffocating
train. She hated these up-country confinements where
there were no conveniences and where it was often hard
to get hold of the doctor if anything went wrong. Most
likely, too, the M.O. would be an R.A.M.C. man who
knew little about maternity work and cared even less.
The railway carriage was like a moving inferno. Not a
breath of air penetrated the thick wire screens over the
windows. Yet if a screen was raised even an inch, a
barrage of fiery, stinging particles, grit, coal-dust and

innumerable flying insects savagely assaulted the travellers.

The train halted at crowded stations that stank of sweating Asiatic humanity and noisome native cookery, crawled forward, and then halted again. To Nurse Ward it seemed as if the nightmare journey would never end. Certainly, this case was starting under specially unfavourable auspices.

When she at last arrived at her destination there was nothing to raise her spirits. It was all as bad as, or even worse, than she had anticipated. The bungalow was hopelessly primitive, the servants were sulky and stupid, and the doctor (an army man, just as she had expected) had been called out into the jungle and no one seemed to know when he would be back.

To add to all this, the patient herself was oddly unsympathetic, a stiff, unsmiling, un-girlish girl who, though outwardly she was polite enough, gave an impression of inward antagonism. Miss Ward took an instant dislike to her.

The nurse had not been half an hour in the Bryants' bungalow before she decided that there was something 'queer' about the case. There was no trace of that half ghoulish, half joyful atmosphere which she regarded as the proper accompaniment to a birth. There was no stream of feminine friends fussing round the patient with reminiscences and advice. Of course, the station was only a small one, but surely there must be some other Englishwomen in it besides that dull Mrs. Hailes who looked as solemn as a judge and about as likely to make a fuss of anyone!

The layette, too, when she inspected it while she was preparing the bedroom, supported her conviction of 'queerness'. The baby clothes were adequate, just enough of each thing and no more, the little garments were neatly if rather amateurishly made; but somehow they failed to convey that sense of loving anticipation which even the most inexpert of sewing mothers usually managed to impart to their work. That round, native-woven basket would make a practical and hygienic container for the infant's toilet articles; the simple, folding canvas cradle was cool and sensible. But Nurse Ward hankered after muslin-draped Treasure Cots, and hampers lined with pale blue or pink silk. It was very strange that not a single gift for the coming child appeared to have arrived from England. Her other patients, even the young wives of hard-up junior officers, had always received a few luxuries, presents from affectionate mothers and relatives at home.

The patient, when finally Josephine Ward got her into bed, failed completely to display that flattering, timorous helplessness, that appreciative dependence upon her ministrations, which Nurse Ward enjoyed. She did not ask a lot of frightened questions as one would expect a girl about to have her first baby to do. Instead, she suffered every physical indignity with a species of dumb resentment that was absolutely impenetrable, refusing to relax for an instant, refusing to respond to any overture, and finally, when the pains got severe, apparently concentrating all her will power in a determination not to utter a sound. The nurse grew quite alarmed at this excessive control, and suggested to the husband that he should try and persuade his wife to behave more normally since she herself could not shake the patient's obstinacy.

Mr. Bryant was the one bright spot in the situation from Josephine Ward's point of view. Such a pleasant, friendly young man, she really felt sorry for him being married to that stuck-up, cold-blooded creature. Yet he seemed devoted to her.

'Don't be too brave, darling,' he said, kneeling beside the bed and kissing her hand; and the nurse had seen tears in his eyes. Anyone but Mrs. Bryant would have been touched.

And later on, when he said shakily: 'If it comes to a choice between my wife and the baby, Nurse, I want you to understand that Celia must be saved at all costs,' it had been quite moving. Yet it was just after this that the patient had insisted that he should be sent away, saying that he got on her nerves. Well, perhaps he was better out of the way for his own sake. Nurse Ward sent him to the doctor's bungalow, although word had already been left for the M.O. to come round as soon as he returned.

Needless to say, the medical man was late in putting in an appearance. Just as she had anticipated, he would leave her to do all the work and then stroll in at the last moment to claim the credit of the delivery for himself. It really was too much, having to cope with the case all alone in the murderous heat with no assistant but a frightened ayah who was more of a trouble than a help. The air itself seemed to drip sweat on to her, every garment she wore was sticking clammily to her flesh. The petrol lamp, a flaring great lantern of a thing, which she had been obliged to bring close to the bed in order to see what she was doing, was like a malodorous furnace at her elbow.

Yes, it was too bad to leave her on her own like this — it should not be expected of her — it was not what she had bargained for when she came out East. Fortunately the case was quite a straightforward one; the girl seemed healthy and strong; there was no sign of any complication. Still, you could never be quite sure with a first child — especially without an X-ray or a proper preliminary examination. What a job! Why had she ever let herself in for this sort of thing when she might have been working in a comfortable office at home with fixed hours, ten to six?

This baby was coming along much too fast now. What was needed was a whiff of chloroform to slow things up: there'd be a nasty tear otherwise. 'Oh, well, it's not my fault,' she thought crossly. 'I've done my best — nobody could have done more.'

A distant vision of the moment, still hours away probably, when she would at last be able to creep under her mosquito net and lie down to rest, passed tantalizingly before her. 'The quicker it comes the sooner things will be over — that's one consolation,' she thought to herself, labouring on stickily and mechanically in the oven-like tropical night.

Just as matters were reaching a climax the doctor arrived. Josephine Ward was so fully occupied, trying, as she would have expressed it, to do the work of three pairs of hands at the same time, that she did not hear him until he was actually in the room. The first intimation she received of his presence was the noise of the door opening, followed by an indifferent masculine voice saying:

'Take it out, Nurse.'

'So you've condescended to turn up, m'lord, have you!' she said to herself with the utmost indignation, thinking simultaneously that it was exactly what she had expected. 'Very nicely timed, I'm sure!'

She did not even look round, but gave an angry snort through her thin nose as she went on delivering the child. The cheek of the man, walking in casually like that when he was too late to be any use, and speaking to her in that tone of voice! 'Take it out, Nurse,' indeed!

XIII

THE words, 'Take it out, Nurse', which Josephine Ward found so offensive, also penetrated the pain cloud surrounding her patient.

For an immeasurable period of time, hours, days, weeks, it seemed, Celia had been struggling against tides of anguish, sinking deeper and deeper into a dreadful sea, whose waves broke at ever shorter intervals until at last there was no respite, but an endless torment that drowned and broke and shattered her to nothing. There was no longer any such person as Celia Bryant in the living world. All that remained was an anonymous hulk, a bleeding rag of flesh in a universe of pain. Her brain had long ago ceased to function. Only somewhere, at the centre of torture, an inexorable core of consciousness persisted.

Hours ago, years ago, she had thought: 'This is too much. No one could bear such agony and go on living.' It seemed that something in her *must* break; that she must either die or fall into oblivion. Yet somehow she had gone on bearing everything. She had not died. She had not lost consciousness. All that she had lost was the sense of her own personal integrity. As a human being she was obliterated; her mind was dispersed. She could not any longer envisage an end of torment. 'Not only not to hope: not even to wait. Just to endure.'

At last, in some region utterly remote, a new thing came into being, words were spoken, and strangely, incredibly, the words had significance. That which had once been Celia could not grasp their meaning because somewhere else a woman's voice was crying out lamentably. Nevertheless, she heard a man speaking, and with a new searing pain there pierced her also a thin shaft of hope, the first premonitory pang of deliverance.

Thereafter she seemed to fall into a black and quiet place, a dark hole of oblivion, where she lay as at the bottom of a deep well. Slowly, painfully, the disintegrated fragments of her being reassembled themselves. By long and difficult stages she returned to some sort of normality. Her brain, her senses, all the strained mechanism of her body and mind, reluctantly began to function once more. The miracle for which she no longer hoped had actually come to pass: there was an end of pain.

She became aware of the heat and glare of the petrol lamp, of the familiar room and of people moving about. Everything was small and remote as if seen through the wrong end of a telescope. There were voices, and a sound she had never heard before — the queer, mewing wail of the new-born. None of these things seemed to concern her: she lay submerged in the lethargy of utter exhaustion.

A face which she dimly recognized bent over her and she heard the doctor's voice speaking again. Isolated words impinged on her consciousness like small, distant explosions, the *crack-crack* of rifle shots far away. 'Tear . . . put in a few stitches . . . hurt —' Once more there was pain; but this time it was nothing — it was ridiculous to call it by the same name as that which had gone before. By contrast with the previous anguish this sharp, stinging sensation was almost pleasurable.

Another dark gulf of unmeasured time followed. Then something was disturbing her with irritating persistence, like a fly settling on her again and again. The nurse was remaking the bed, changing the sheets, slipping a clean nightdress over her head. Celia felt weakly resentful: why couldn't she be left in peace? The woman brought something red and white and held it before her. 'A little girl,' she was saying.

Celia distantly observed the inchoate features, the quivering, stick-like arms. This was the thing that had torn itself out of her body, that had weighed her down for so many tedious months. She groped feebly in her heart and in her mind for some sort of response. There was none. She felt absolutely nothing about it. The little red mommet was nothing to do with her; it was even less connected with her than was the garment it wore, the shirt which had seemed so absurdly small when she sewed it and which she now saw was actually too large for its wearer.

She perceived that her husband was also beside her. His agreeable, boyish face, moist with heat and emotion, hung over her. His eyes, which always reminded her of the lustrous, sentimental eyes of a prize spaniel, were brimming with tears. 'He hasn't suffered anything — why is he crying?' she wondered with weariness and a certain remote curiosity. He, too, was talking about the child — 'Our own little daughter' — and beaming at her affectionately through his tears.

Celia forced herself to smile. All her nerves seemed twisted like over-taut strings suddenly loosened, every muscle felt bruised. She was profoundly indifferent to Clare, to the infant, to everything. But she could not dissociate herself from the world any longer. Returning vitality dragged her back into the midst of these circumstances which still seemed not to concern her. The smile

72

was difficult to achieve, like lifting a heavy weight. Clare was delighted to see it.

'Celia . . . my darling . . . I'm so, so happy,' he was repeating over and over again.

She looked at him attentively for a moment and then closed her eyes. She knew that she ought to speak to him, but the effort was too great and she could not think of anything to say. Under the sheet she moved her hand slowly down her body. Her stomach was flat and private again. She kept her hand on it. She had the sensation of appreciating her body for the first time. It was her own now. The nightmare was over. 'Never again!' she thought. She felt that she had been deeply wronged because no one had made her understand the horror of birth. 'Mother ought to have told me how terrible it was. She had Harold and me . . . She couldn't possibly have forgotten —'

She opened her eyes again. Clare was still bending over her.

'Speak to me, Celia! Say something!' he implored her wistfully.

What was there to say? An echo in her mind blankly repeated, 'Say something!'

She moved her lips. Perhaps she was going to say, 'Everything's all right, Clare' — she knew that she ought to reassure him — but just at that moment she saw a strange native woman moving about the room.

'Who's that?' she asked in a voice that had to be summoned laboriously through clogging weakness.

Her husband explained that the stranger was a female sweeper who had come specially to destroy the afterbirth. No member of any other caste was allowed to touch it as it was considered unclean.

73

Celia did not say anything more. Presently she was left alone in the dark. Under the sheet she lay as straight and still as if she were in her coffin, not sleeping, but hearing like the monotonous reiteration of an imaginary brain-fever bird the two words, 'never again'.

TWO

THE train service from London to Jessington was very good. Nearly all the big expresses for Birmingham and Wolverhampton stopped there and the journey took under two hours. Because the trains were so frequent they were rarely crowded. Celia had a carriage to herself on this stormy March afternoon. As the train unobtrusively moved out of Paddington station she closed the sliding door between the corridor and her compartment. Jessington was the first stop. Nobody would disturb her now. Not that anyone would be likely to come into the carriage with *that*, anyhow, unless the train were packed full, she thought, looking at the bamboo basket on the seat opposite.

In this basket, that was now slightly battered after weeks of travel, Celia's infant daughter had slept through most of her six thousand mile journey. She was asleep now. Celia moved a fold of the shawl a little and looked at the placid face of the five-months-old baby.

She looked at it quite impersonally as she might have looked at a strange child placed in her charge. She was remembering how fond the stewardess on the boat who had helped her to care for the baby had grown of the child, and how she had nearly cried when the voyage ended and it was time for them to part. 'If a stranger could feel like that about her, why don't I feel more?' she wondered. It was strange, she had never been able to think of the baby as really being *hers*. It was just a child which, by some weird accident, she had been instrumental in bringing into the world. There seemed to be no closer connection between them. She felt no connection in her blood. The stewardess had seen a resemblance between mother and daughter. Celia looked at her child closely, seeking the likeness which she could never discover.

The round head with its delicate fluff of downy, almost white hair gave a first impression of pathetic vulnerability. But a more attentive inspection revealed something much more forceful in the tiny creature: an absolutely indomitable will to exist. The very way she slept through all the clattering disturbances of travel expressed a mindless determination. Even the roundness of the head really had a suggestion of strength. A tremendous natural force, unconscious, impersonal and ruthless, controlled all the infantile actions. There was something almost terrifying in the implacable way the embryonic being exacted nourishment, warmth and attention, no matter what tragedies or vicissitudes might affect its supporters. 'How *tough* babies are,' Celia thought, readjusting the shawl.

The child had not stirred. She was fast asleep and would probably sleep all the way to Jessington, lulled by the steady roar and motion of the speeding train.

From the opposite corner, Celia continued to stare absentmindedly at the basket and the white cocoon-shape inside it. 'Is there something wrong — unnatural — about me?' It was a question she had often asked herself before. 'Perhaps if she'd been born under different conditions I should have felt fonder of her,' her thoughts wandered on. 'If she'd been born in a nursing home and I'd had chloroform . . . But that's nonsense — women never had anaesthetics when they had babies until quite recently. It can't be anything to do with that. Is it because I'm only nineteen — not really old enough to want a baby? But it can't be anything to do with that, either, because lots of girls of nineteen do have children and love them very much. No, it's something in me that's queer . . . I didn't want a child at all to begin with, of course: perhaps that made a difference. But Winifred Hailes told me I should love it once it arrived . . . And I believed her. I quite expected to love it . . . But somehow the love never came. I wonder why?'

The train raced on across the sombre landscape. Outside the walls of the swaying carriage stretched the fields, woods, small hills, towns, and villages of England. Although it was March the country still seemed locked in winter. The trees were leafless, the fields of grass or damp ploughing had a derelict air under the chilly grey sky where rooks were rising in eddies that looked like winter. It was growing dusk and a cold, metallic streak ripped the clouds in the west. The woodwork of the carriage creaked, the train wheels drummed out their monotonous rhythm, there was a stuffy smell of upholstery and steam heating. Celia did not feel like a traveller returning home. It all seemed familiar to her, commonplace, almost as if she had never been away.

She had nothing to read and her thoughts drifted into a dreamy retrospect, influenced by her previous musings about little Clare. Clare! The other Clare had not wanted the baby girl to be called by his name. He would have chosen a more romantic, more feminine name for the little creature. But Celia had decided from the first to call the child after her husband. Clare was one of the few names you could give to either a boy or a girl. She was particularly glad now that she had kept to her decision. In some un-thought-out way she had felt that she was paying a tribute to the young man by insisting that his daughter

79

should be called after him. She had wanted to make some appreciative gesture towards him. He had always been kind and generous and friendly to her. Poor Clare! It was not his fault that she had never been able to make the ultimate response to his affection, that some secret inner door had always remained closed to him.

She remembered the time after the birth of the child when she had seemed to come nearer to Clare Bryant than ever before. During those days of physical weakness he had supported her unfailingly, endlessly warm-hearted, patient and understanding. She had felt the cold heart of reserve melting in her; she had felt that she almost loved him, almost loved the child. Her husband's devotion seemed to envelop the three of them in a comforting warmth. For the first time she felt herself really a woman.

Did all women experience that warm, peaceful, gentle feeling after they had given birth to a child? Was it just part of the biological bag of tricks? It had seemed so safe and simple and normal to relax in that aura of protected love; not troubling about one's mind or about anything except the fulfilment of one's female destiny. How long would that contentment have lasted? If things had turned out differently, would she have spent the rest of her life with Clare in that state of mild, restful affection, being a good wife and mother?

The train was beginning to slow down. In a few moments now it would be running into Jessington. Peering through the windows into the thickening dusk Celia could see an outline she recognized: the spire of Saint Andrew's church pointing like a stern admonitory finger above the water meadows.

She put on her hat which she had taken off at Paddington and got her suitcase down from the rack. 'It'll soon be starting now,' she thought, without being quite clear what she meant. Desborough House was coming nearer, she was conscious of a dark, depressing influence stretching tentacles to meet her from which she would find it hard to escape. She knew what was before her, but a secret spring of confidence, of excitement, made dejection seem distant and unimportant like a thundercloud far away.

The train stopped in the station. An elderly man in a black overcoat stepped forward in front of the lights and the coloured blur of magazines on the bookstall. Her father: how stiff and inaccessible he looked in his black coat and bowler hat! Her carriage had stopped almost precisely opposite him, and before she had time to open the door he had opened it himself with a large, capable hand, and the voice which had chilled her so many times all through her childhood with its polite indifference was saying:

'How are you, Celia? Your mother and I have both been most grieved — ' The bristly moustache brushed her cheek.

THE day after Celia's return to Desborough House was Sunday, a day to which Mrs. Henzell always looked forward. In the extremely circumscribed life that she led, the invalid's life which relies for its interest upon trivial variations hardly noticeable to the robust, the first day of the week stood out with agreeable distinctness from the rest.

Sundays were characterized by several domestic happenings which did not take place on any other day. To begin with, Mattie brought up her breakfast half an hour later than usual. When she had finished her lightly boiled egg, her toast and marmalade and her two cups of weak China tea, Marion Henzell liked to potter about her bedroom for a long time, looking through her chest-of-drawers and inspecting the hoard of miscellaneous articles — odds and ends of ribbon, cardboard boxes, tissue paper and so on — which she kept at the back of the wardrobe. There was no real reason why she should not do this every day of her life if she so desired: yet Sunday was the only morning when she could allow herself to dawdle about upstairs with a clear conscience. Mattie and the cook between them were really responsible for the running of the household. But Mrs. Henzell, although finally she left everything in their hands, nevertheless felt obliged to spend an hour in the kitchen each morning, occupying herself ineffectively with superfluous tasks and giving incomplete or contradictory orders in her thin, chirruping voice. Only on Sundays was she exempt from the self-imposed duty: all household arrangements had then been made the previous day, the meals were ordered, no tradesmen came to the door.

While she slowly dressed she would listen to the church bells, and, if she felt specially well, she would play with the idea of accompanying her husband to the eleven o'clock service, although it was years since she had done such a thing and she knew perfectly well that she had no intention of doing so to-day. The peal of bells would be followed by the single last five-minute bell, the front door would close with its muffled thud as the lawyer set out with his prayer book and closely rolled silk umbrella. Mrs. Henzell always felt a slight, unacknowledged relief when he had left the house. It would seem to her that the temperature had suddenly risen by a few degrees. She would put on one or other of her two 'best' dresses — the fine black wool in winter, the grey-and-white patterned voile if it were summer time — and proceed downstairs.

Next, during the six months between September and April, came the lighting of the drawing-room fire, followed, winter and summer alike, by the most important sabbatical ceremony — the drinking of a glass of sherry when the head of the house returned from church. The climax of the day would now have been reached, but there was still the minor interest of the midday joint. The circumstance of sitting in the drawing-room, too, had a pleasant novelty, for the big room, so little frequented, had acquired a kind of glamour in the eyes of its mistress and every object it contained was endowed with the charm of the unfamiliar.

The aura of this particular Sunday, however, Marion Henzell was unable to savour in her usual leisurely way. All the time she was eating her breakfast, all the time she was dressing and doing her hair, she was conscious of an uncomfortable sensation. As she opened one drawer after another, she was not really looking at the contents but wondering what Celia was doing.

How much was Celia's arrival going to disturb the domestic routine? She had always been rather a disturbing influence. And now there was this baby as well. A baby at Desborough House! It was utterly incongruous — revolutionary — Mrs. Henzell felt her heart gripped with an apprehensive qualm whenever she thought of it. And yet, of course, Celia and the child had to be there. There was nowhere else for them to go. 'Fortunately she has her home to come to,' Frederick had said in his conclusive manner when they had first had the bad news.

Mrs. Henzell folded a flowered scarf which she had not worn since her son's death and which she would never wear again, and put it back in the drawer. She could no longer spin out the pretence that this was an ordinary Sunday morning. She must go and talk to her daughter; sympathize with her, solicit her confidence. Last night there had been little time for conversation. In the bustle of arrival, unpacking and putting the baby to bed the evening seemed to have flown.

She went out on to the landing. The five-minute church bell was ringing its monotonous, unmusical *clang-clang-clang*. In the past Celia had always gone to church with her father; would she go to-day? But no, of course she would have to stay and look after little Clare. How difficult it was to remember, to adjust oneself to the idea of a child in the house. Was it possible that Frederick would interrupt his routine sufficiently to stay at home on account of Celia's arrival? Just at this moment came the muted clap of the front door, louder out here than it sounded in the bedroom. The solicitor had departed as usual.

84

Mrs. Henzell put her hand on the knob of Celia's door. As the door was opening a doubt pricked her. Ought she to have knocked? One could hardly enter the room occupied by a married woman and her child in the same informal way that one went into a schoolgirl's bedroom. On the other hand, Celia was still only nineteen and her own daughter into the bargain. Uncertainty accentuated the peevish lines on her face as she struggled with this dilemma — the first, she pessimistically surmised, of many similar tiresome complications. She had already forgotten that she had come with the intention of being sympathetic.

Celia was sitting on a chair with the child on her knee. The small, high room seemed full of the baby's belongings, there was a faint, indescribable nursery odour that came to the elder woman like the ghost of a lost memory. She glanced round with puckered eyes at the room, avoiding the two pairs of human eyes fastened upon her.

She noticed that the bed was made and that the general disorder was only superficial; and for some reason this evidence of her daughter's efficiency in a situation where she herself would have been surrounded by chaos, gave her a sense of grievance.

'Celia, I didn't think of it last night, but perhaps it would be better if you moved into one of the larger bed-rooms — ? You're rather cramped in here now.'

'No, thanks, Mother. This is quite all right. I haven't had time yet to get things straight — that's why the room seems so crowded.' Celia stood up, holding the baby against her shoulder. 'Clare's just finished her feed. We're rather late this morning. Will you keep an eye on her while I wash the bottle in the bathroom?'

Marion Henzell felt as if the scene were taking place

in a dream instead of in a bedroom of her own house. She looked at her creation, the slim, pale-faced girl with bright hair, and felt that she was confronting a stranger. Celia apparently took it for granted that her mother would do as she had just asked. She began to hold the child out towards her, changed her mind, and laid her down on the bed.

'She'll be quite safe there — just see that she doesn't roll off,' she said, as she carried the empty feeding bottle out of the room.

Mrs. Henzell stood nervously beside her grandchild. A ray of pale March sunshine entered the window and fell on the pretty, fair-haired baby who smiled and stretched out her hands in one of those touchingly confiding gestures which are among the strongest defences of children.

'Poor little mite,' murmured the woman, and her expression relaxed, growing softer and less self-absorbed. She bent down and touched Clare on the cheek with one dry, wrinkled finger. The child was startled and made a protesting sound, screwing up her pink features. The grandmother immediately drew back in alarm, her faint outward impulse of love quickly lost in the vague personal apprehensions of the neurotic.

Celia came back and picked up the child.

'I thought I'd put her basket into the conservatory this morning,' she said. 'To-morrow I must buy a pram so that she can sleep out in the garden.'

A LITTLE before twelve o'clock mother and daughter were sitting in the drawing-room. The fire, lighted a quarter of an hour earlier, was burning up well, transparent sunshine came in through the windows, and the room did not feel too cold. Mrs. Henzell was reading the gospel for the day from a book in a soft black leather cover that was worn almost purple with use. Every few lines her attention wandered, and she glanced surreptitiously over the top of her glasses at Celia who was sitting on the opposite side of the fireplace sewing something for the child.

Marion Henzell felt ill at ease in the company of her daughter. She still had the sensation of sharing the room with a stranger. What was the girl thinking about? Once more she felt that she ought to sympathize with her, to say something intimate, to have a heart-to-heart talk with her now that they were alone. Yet it seemed impossible to approach her. Questions, a certain question in particular, which a nervous self-consciousness prevented her from uttering, kept coming into her head. She tried in vain to frame an opening sentence.

Gradually a sense of suppressed indignation took possession of her. Why didn't Celia make things easy and natural? Why didn't she meet her half way by making an advance on her side? Next time she glanced at the girl she was conscious of disapproval. There was something unsuitable in her attitude. Celia did not look sad. Certainly she did not look gay, either. Her face was perfectly composed, neutral; and every now and then she would drop her sewing and gaze into the fire where the clear flames were briskly attacking the still un-reddened coal. Each time she did this her expression altered, a dreamy, indecipherable look came on her face, almost as if she were brooding over a secret. She did not look like a mourner. A thought suddenly struck Mrs. Henzell.

'Haven't you got anything black to wear?' she inquired.

'No. This is almost the only warm dress I've got.' Celia stopped her work and looked meditatively at the dress she was wearing which was made of wool; a soft, smoky blue-grey with buttons down the front. 'I only had thin clothes with me, and of course there were no shops out there where you could buy anything decent. I'll get something black to-morrow if you think it's really necessary.'

Mrs. Henzell closed her book after inserting between its pages a marker of purple satin ribbon embroidered in silver thread with a cross. The words 'if you think it's really necessary' struck her as showing a scandalous lack of proper feeling — of being, in fact, in very bad taste — but before she was able to think of an adequate remonstrative answer her thoughts were deflected by the appearance of Mattie.

The old servant plodded forward with a tray bearing the decanter of sherry and five glasses which she set down on a round table of inlaid wood in the middle of the room. Her mistress counted the glasses.

'*Five* glasses, Mattie?' she exclaimed in an astonished tone.

'The master told me just before he went out that most likely he would be bringing Mr. and Mrs. Marriott in with him after church.'

Mrs. Henzell was thrown into an immediate flutter

of agitation by this piece of news which Mattie communicated with her customary stolidity.

'The Marriotts coming . . .! Why was I not told before so that I should have been prepared instead of having it sprung on me at the last moment . . .? Yes, I suppose they would want to hear — '

Her eyes again rested upon her daughter as the consoling thought, 'They won't be able to stop long on account of lunch time', flashed through her mind, to be followed by one less satisfactory:

'Mrs. Marriott will think it most extraordinary to see you in that blue dress — What can we do about it? I know — You must wear my black jacket . . . That will be better than nothing.'

She went out of the room and presently came back with a short black knitted coat. The girl passively accepted it from her mother and pushed her strong arms into the sleeves. She had an air of submitting to everything with docile indifference and the hint of a smile in her secretive eyes which gave no clue to her real thoughts. The jacket was too small for her and smelt strongly of camphor balls. When she had put it on she looked all at once extremely young, quite childish, with the somewhat pitiful charm of a little girl 'dressing up'. Even Mrs. Henzell was affected, though she did not realize what it was that recalled to her the idea of saying something consolatory. Her lips started to shape the question she had all the time been wanting to ask, but before any sound came Celia spoke. It appeared that she also wanted to ask a question.

'Could Mattie look after Clare for an hour this afternoon, do you think, Mother? There's nothing to do, really. She's very good. She'll just sleep or play quietly in her basket. I'll give her her two-o'clock bottle before I go

89

out and I'll be back long before it's time to put her to bed.'

Mrs. Henzell could hardly believe that she had heard aright. Her face slowly changed to a mask of horror-stricken amazement as the full meaning of the words dawned upon her.

'You want to go out somewhere this afternoon — ?'

'Yes. A friend — someone I met on the boat who lives not far from here — is coming to take me out for a drive in his car.'

'Celia! What are you saying . . .? You've arranged all this . . . without consulting us . . . You only arrived last night, and to-day you are going out . . . with a *man* — so soon — after what has happened. Have you no sense of . . . decency . . . or . . .? What will your father say?'

Marion Henzell suddenly raised her hands and pressed them against her temples. It seemed to her for a moment that the room had vanished and that she herself was not really there either but lost in a bad dream. She took an uncertain step forward. Her eyes had a tearful bewildered look. Celia came up and touched her on the shoulder.

'Don't look so worried, Mother. There's nothing wrong about it. There's no reason why I shouldn't have friends, you know. Clare wouldn't want me to be without friends.' She seemed to be on the verge of saying something further, but changed her mind and became silent.

Mrs. Henzell felt for her handkerchief and tremblingly wiped away a tear. The phrases just spoken had not re-assured her. They had sounded cool, indifferent, deter-mined. They made her feel that something strange and alarming and uncontrollable had come into her sheltered life. She felt a frightened longing to throw herself upon the familiar support of her husband.

Just then the door opened and a stout elderly lady in a sealskin coat bustled into the room. She went at once to Celia and embraced her warmly in a bear-like hug. The girl smiled, and her expression softened. It was the first spontaneous sign of affection she had received in Jessington.

'My poor child! We have come at once to offer our deepest sympathy — such a terrible loss! How you must have suffered! He was almost like a son to me, you know, so I can understand a little of what you feel.'

Mrs. Marriott kept one arm round Celia's shoulders as she was speaking. The girl relaxed luxuriously for a few seconds against that motherly support. To her surprise she felt the prick of tears in her eyes although she was not thinking of Clare but of the softness of the fur sleeve that had brushed her cheek and of the tender, fresh, spring-like scent of the bunch of violets which the visitor had pinned to her coat.

The two men came in from the hall where they had paused to remove their overcoats. Mr. Marriott was shaking his head and muttering, 'A bad business, a bad business', under his breath. In the general greetings Celia's composure returned. She found herself once more standing alone and detached from the scene. Frederick Henzell observed that his wife was distressed.

'You look upset, my dear. Hadn't you better sit down?' he remarked, at the same time going to the table and starting to pour the wine into the glasses.

'Of course she's upset!' cried Mrs. Marriott, drowning the other woman's inarticulate murmur. 'It's been a dreadful shock to us all. A most terrible thing — a disaster. And to think that only eighteen months have gone by since — ' She interrupted herself to accept a glass of sherry which the lawyer carried over to her. 'Give Celia a glass,' she went on. 'That's right. Fill it up to the brim. She needs it, poor child. How thin and pale she's looking! And the little baby, the darling — shall we be able to peep at her? Little Clare ... Such a touching thought to call her after the poor, dear boy.'

The good lady gave a deep sigh that was plainly audible to everyone. Her voluble, kindly voice seemed to fill the room. Marion Henzell sat silently by the fire, with bowed head, holding a handkerchief to her cheek. Every now and then she shuddered, and the straggling wisps of hair stirred on her neck. The lawyer devoted himself to Mr. Marriott. They stood together near the round table and talked gravely in undertones. Celia opened her mouth with its firm, well-curved lips and slowly sipped from her glass. Her father suddenly spoke to her.

'No one wants to cause you unnecessary pain, Celia,' he said, speaking as clearly and tonelessly as usual, 'but I think that you should try to tell us a little more about this very sad event. You must remember that we know nothing except the bare fact of your husband's death. I say nothing about ourselves, but Mrs. Marriott, as his sole living relative, is naturally entitled to a few details.'

Both the Marriotts nodded their heads: the husband in sad confirmation, the wife with an air of mournful fortitude. Mrs. Henzell also looked up. It was the question which she had lacked sufficient courage to ask.

Celia put down her glass. A chilly feeling came over her. She frowned and looked at the carpet where the sun was outlining each thread of the pile with a tiny halo of dust.

'I wasn't there; I don't know any details. All I know is what I told you in my letter. Clare was travelling on the engine, inspecting the flooded line. Part of the track had been washed away, the engine turned over and he was killed. Nobody else except the native fireman was hurt.'

Her voice sounded dull, almost sullen. She suddenly felt overwhelmed with animosity, not only towards Desborough House, but also for the cold blue sky outside the window, for the violets on Mrs. Marriott's breast, and for the inquisitive way in which everybody, she fancied, was staring at her.

'What right have they to question me?' she thought gloomily. 'It's nothing to do with them. They don't care about Clare being dead, and they don't care about me, either.'

There was an unexpected sound from the conservatory. The baby had woken up and was starting to whimper.

'That's Clare — I must go to her,' Celia said. She was glad of the excuse to escape, and hurried out of the room without looking back.

SHORTLY before lunch-time the visitors departed, and punctually at one o'clock Mattie carried the joint of hot roast beef to the dining-room table, exactly as if it had been an ordinary Sunday. Just as if it had been an ordinary Sunday, too, Mr. Henzell drew the blade of the already sharp knife downwards over the steel two or three times before he started to carve the meat. He was alone at the table. Celia was detained by the needs of the baby, and Mrs. Henzell had retired to her bedroom with a headache. The combined excitements of the Marriott's visit and of her daughter's subversive behaviour had proved too much for the nerves of the invalid. She had not felt equal to imparting Celia's announcement to her husband, but, overcome by a state of affairs altogether beyond her, had taken refuge in her familiar sanctuary of illness.

The solicitor was too accustomed to these sudden nervous attacks to pay them any special attention. In the absence of his wife and daughter, he carved himself two slices of beef, took a spoonful of cabbage and a spoonful of roast potatoes, and calmly began his meal.

His mind, however, was not quite as calm as usual. He was worried about Celia's affairs, the girl seemed fated to be a trouble to him: her presence in the house was disturbing and he considered that she was not displaying at all a proper spirit. If she had seemed prostrated by grief he could have made allowances for her; but, on the contrary, she appeared to be almost callous. The way she had spoken in the drawing-room just now had really been most unbecoming. His thick eyebrows met in a frown as his knife took up some mustard from the edge of his plate and smeared it over a forkful of beef. How extraordinarily unfortunate it was that young Bryant should have got himself killed like that! Frederick Henzell felt aggrieved, almost as if the young man had done something discreditable in dying. It was too bad that he, the lawyer, should get his daughter back on his hands after only a year and a half of marriage: and with a baby, into the bargain. What a perpetual problem the girl was! She was difficult and intractable and everything connected with her seemed to go wrong.

Before long the object of his meditations appeared. Celia apologized for being late and laid a cutting from a newspaper beside her father's plate before she went to her chair. He glanced at the cutting which he saw was printed on thin paper from a foreign journal and contained a brief account of the death of the young engineer. Having grasped these facts, he carved a slice from the cooling joint and handed it to his daughter. Neither of them made any comment. Celia ate quickly to catch up with her father who had already nearly finished his first course. The negligent way she put the good food into her mouth was displeasing to him, but he disguised his annoyance, sitting stiff and controlled until her plate was empty. Then he rang the bell for the apple-pie which was cut and eaten in silence.

Directly the meal was over, Celia went upstairs to attend to her child. The lawyer carried the newspaper cutting into the drawing-room. The fire had died down, but it would not be replenished; it had done its work of airing the room for the week. The sun had moved away from the windows and the atmosphere felt gloomy and cold. The tray with the decanter and the empty glasses had been removed.

Frederick Henzell sat down in the chair which earlier in the day had been occupied by his wife. He unfolded the cutting, carefully smoothing out the creases in the thin, inferior paper against his knee. Then he put on his glasses and attentively read through the paragraphs which some unknown, insignificant journalist had written in a florid Eurasian style describing the tragedy of his son-in-law. When he had assimilated the information contained in the cutting he refolded it and put it away in his pocket. For a minute or so he sat frowning at the dying fire. Then he reached for the *Observer* which Mattie had left on a table beside him and started to read the leading article.

After about half an hour he put the Sunday paper aside. There was no doubt about it, this business of Celia's was very unsettling. He felt restless, and decided to go and inquire after his wife's headache. When he was in the hall, his daughter came downstairs in her hat and coat. He was very surprised to see her dressed to go out.

'Where are you going?'

'I'm going out for a drive with a friend.'

'You're going for a drive!'

'Yes,' Celia answered, as though the statement were perfectly natural and ordinary.

'And who is this friend, may I ask?'

'His name is Anthony Bonham. We met on the boat coming home. It's quite all right . . . I told mother I was going . . . and Mattie doesn't mind looking after Clare for an hour or so till I come back.' Her voice was as quiet and cool as if she were speaking of some everyday matter which had been discussed and decided long ago.

The solicitor stood speechless.

'I'm probably going to marry Anthony,' Celia added calmly, as she passed him and let herself out of the front door.

THE door closed behind her and Celia walked rapidly away. 'Well, that's done it,' she thought as she hurried up the drive, half afraid that her father might emerge and recall her. 'Why did I say anything about marriage?' she next thought. She had not intended to mention the possibility; at any rate, not until she had seen Anthony again. Suppose he had altered his mind? Suppose his family had persuaded him to give her up? With a superstition that had no real place in her nature, but which was a manifestation of emotional stress, she began to fear that misfortune would fall upon her as a result of her incautious words. 'I ought never to have spoken about it.' It was the cold, repressive atmosphere of Desborough House that had antagonized her into giving utterance to what should have remained secret. She looked over her shoulder. The house with its narrow turret looked like the outlying wing of an institution, a gloomy hospital or a penitentiary. The aspect of the closed door suggested incarceration.

As soon as she had turned the bend of the drive and the house was hidden from her, Celia felt better. She had only said what had to be said sometime; it was a good thing to have got it over. Suddenly her parents seemed unimportant. What did it matter what they thought or said? They meant nothing to her, no more than the tiny brownish-white florets on the lauristinus which she was just passing. They had never wanted her; she had never occupied any real place in their lives; Desborough House had never seemed like her real home. Now she was going to meet the man she loved, walking towards him in the blustery March wind — and he alone was important. Even if he did not want to marry her after all, she would not go on living at Desborough House. How could she ever have contemplated such a possibility? During the independent months she had been away she had changed, but the Jessington household remained static, and now it was intolerable to her. 'I'd forgotten how depressing it was — so full of unhappiness and disapproval — I could never live there again. I'd rather scrub floors — anything.'

The thought of the dead Clare was also accompanying her as she walked, but far off, on the outskirts of her mind, like a dog that, knowing itself unwanted, still persists in following its master at a distance, keeping half out of sight. Now she called the thought to her, as it were, that by admitting its presence she might banish it. What senseless accidents controlled the destinies of human beings! Clare had been a harmless creature who enjoyed life. If he had not chosen to ride on the engine over that particular stretch of the line on that particular day, he would be living now, and she would never have so much as heard of Anthony Bonham. The face of Clare, dim, with sad, lustrous eyes, floated before her, a reproachful, unlucky ghost, and then sank back into the ocean of the past.

She had reached the end of the drive where a pair of tall, solid wooden gates stood between her and the public road. These gates were always kept shut, a small door having been cut in one of them for the use of people on foot. As she was about to lift the latch of this door something made her look back.

The drive curved away, sloping gently down towards the hidden house and the river. High, black-looking evergreens stood on each side with no crocuses at their feet. The drive was the colour of lead, the earth was barren and black with snake-like roots here and there, the dark trees looked like executioners. 'I'm glad I'm going to meet Anthony outside. I couldn't bear him to come to the house,' she thought, as she stepped through the narrow opening into the road.

She walked on in the direction from which he must come. No one was about on Sunday afternoon in this quiet residential neighbourhood. On each side were high hedges or walls over which appeared the branches of trees with large swelling buds. Here and there a flowering tree was in bloom, lifting delicate pink or white sprays which scattered their fragile confetti at each gust of wind. Thin clouds were piling up like a heap of plates in the sky. There was a smell of rising sap and of freshly turned earth from the gardens.

Celia was staring ahead with intense anticipation. Her eyes under the blue sky were bluer than usual; the peculiar blue of wood-smoke rising on a still day. 'Supposing he doesn't come?' she murmured under her breath, and the words seemed to fall back like cold drops on her heart. She walked faster. Her eyes were concentrated as if in an effort to pierce the intervening houses, hills and trees with their imperative gaze. Suddenly a strange and almost painful sensation passed over her, taking away her breath and sending an electric vibration through her nerves.

A car had come into sight and was approaching her. She instinctively waved her hand. The car slackened speed and pulled up beside her.

The driver was a remarkably handsome young man in the mid twenties. His shoulders were broad, his waist and hips narrow, and there was about him that enviable¹ indefinable air of being thoroughly at home in life which is the happy result of a confident nature combined with certain physical and worldly advantages. The bony structure of his face was good; his expression was sensitive; in later life he might have a distinguished look. But at present some immaturity in his countenance, and particularly the flash of white teeth against his skin when he smiled, gave him a youthful and naive charm. He opened the door of the car and leaned out.

'Celia! How nice of you to come and meet me! I was just wondering if this was the right road for Desborough House.'

She put her foot on the running-board, resting her hand on the open door.

'I couldn't wait for you inside. Everything was so horrid,' she said, bringing out the words with difficulty. Suddenly she looked into his eyes and smiled in a way which translated her to real beauty. 'But it's all right now; nothing matters now that you're here.'

Anthony Bonham took her hands and drew her into the car. He did not understand what caused the emotion in her voice, but the sound of it moved him.

'It's wonderful to see you . . . I'm so awfully glad —'

She sat in the seat beside him. He put his arm round her and kissed her cheek. A breath of bracing March air, of spring, of vitality, came to him from her cold flesh.

'Haven't your people been nice to you?'

Celia shook her head.

'But surely they were pleased to see you again? — pleased about the baby?'

'No. I've told you what it's like in that house, but you'll never understand — nobody could possibly understand without living there. I'd almost forgotten myself — such restriction and unfriendliness all the time . . . They don't want me or baby Clare — we're just a nuisance . . . a burden. And yet they don't want me to have any freedom. They want to stop me doing everything I like doing. If they could, they'd have prevented me from seeing you to-day.'

Her voice shook, her eyes were shining with tears. Suddenly she dropped her head and hid her face against his coat.

'I wish I didn't love you, Anthony. It's dangerous to love anyone so much . . . everyone's trying to separate us. I'm so afraid they'll succeed in the end.'

For a moment she rested against him, abandoned, then sat up and impatiently brushed away the tears that had not had time to fall. The passionate love which she now felt for the first time had altered her face so profoundly that it was almost unrecognizable. It no longer looked neutral and inexpressive, but tender, vivid, intense, with soft parted lips and sparkling eyes. A tremendous force of life, youth, and love seemed to emanate from her. Anthony all at once felt carried away. He put his arms round her and kissed her repeatedly, her neck, her hair and her mouth.

'Have you told them . . .?' he muttered, his lips close to her ear. 'What have you said about me?'

Celia did not answer. The feel of his kisses, the warmth of his breath on her skin, filled her with an emotion so exalted that the trivial act of speech seemed below her notice. Desborough House, her parents, her child, all were unreal, blotted out by the nearness of this man who seemed at the moment to fill the entire universe. The sound of approaching footsteps broke through her ecstatic trance. She drew back and sat stiffly until the stranger had passed. The everyday world reclaimed her.

'And your father?' she asked in a low voice. 'What does he say about it? He's against me, of course? I suppose he's very angry.'

Anthony took her hand, kissed it, and held it against his breast.

'He's a bit difficult. But he'll come round in time. Don't worry — everything will be all right.' The young man suddenly tightened his fingers over her hand with a vehement movement as an obscure emotion gripped his heart, an emotion belonging not to spring, hope and love, but to winter and death.

Perhaps it was a sudden chill in the wind, perhaps a cloud crossing the path of the sun, that conveyed to him like a premonition the sense of inexorably flowing time, and of the precariousness and transience of all lovely things.

'I mustn't lose you,' he murmured, embracing her once more. 'Whatever happens we must be together. You mustn't stay here where people make you unhappy — you must come with me to Stone and we'll never be parted again . . . never . . . never.'

FIFTEEN miles south of Jessington was the village of Stone where the Bonham family had lived for nearly a hundred years. The original baronet was one of those pioneer merchants who received titles as the reward of services rendered to British trade in the East. When he retired, he built for himself the house, Great Stone, which his descendants had inhabited ever since. The family, though wealthy, was quite obscure. The Bonhams were quiet, rather proud people, fond of country life, who lived contentedly on their small, beautifully kept estate. Although they were no longer actively connected with trade, their Eastern interests still brought in plenty of money which they spent mostly at home. They hunted and fished, entertained well but unostentatiously, attended all the balls and race meetings in the vicinity, played tennis and golf, had good taste in dress and knew how to choose a bottle of wine. They were popular with their tenants and dependants as well as with the local gentry. Beyond their own little sphere they were completely unknown.

Stone was outside the area directly affected by the spread of the great industrial towns. Nevertheless, a slow change had imperceptibly been taking place during the last quarter of a century in the life of the countryside. One after another the large houses were changing hands, estates were gradually being broken up, the old order of county society was giving way little by little to a new aristocracy of wealth.

The Bonhams, separated by two generations from their commercial origin, preferred not to mix with the newcomers, and, as a result, their social life had of late years slowly become more restricted. The change was almost unnoticeable, but it was there. The young Bonhams did not visit so many houses as their predecessors had done, they did not go to quite so many dances, they did not entertain so frequently. A new exclusiveness was gradually being thrust upon the family, and with it came an increase in family pride.

Sir Charles Bonham, a widower with two grown-up children, was devoted to his estate. Friends and neighbours might move out of the district, but nothing would induce him to budge from the big, plain, solid brick house which his grandfather had built on the lower slope of the hill which sheltered the village on the south-east. It was not as if the place had come to him out of the blue. He had been born there, had lived there all his life, and knew the history of almost every tree like that of a personal friend. The trees, some of them rare Canadian firs and spruces that did well on those bleak slopes, were his special pride as they had been the pride of his father and grandfather before him.

'I was born in this house and I intend to die here,' he announced from time to time through the years when the departure of yet another acquaintance brought up the subject: 'and I hope my son and his son will live and die here too. Great Stone was built by a Bonham for the Bonhams. It's the only proper place for us. I've planted an avenue of walnuts that my grandchildren will see in their prime.'

The village itself, fortunately, was still quite unspoiled. If old Sir Edward Bonham had been able to revisit the place, he would have noticed very few changes to show for the century that had almost completed itself since his death.

The road which climbed up from the plain to the cluster of red-brown houses did not go any farther but ended in the irregular open space in front of a squat little church guarded by seven enormous yews. Beyond that there was only the narrow private road leading higher up the hill to Great Stone. The big, indestructible-looking house with its fine arched doorway and its double row of tall, gleaming, stone-set windows, dominated the village. It was a landmark, standing out there boldly by itself, unscreened either by creepers or trees. The carefully laid out orchards and plantations had been planned in such a way that they nowhere obstructed the view of the house which sat squarely on a shoulder of unbroken, bright green turf. Each tree, young or old, in its perfection resembled a well-drilled soldier, a member of a disciplined body deployed in a strategic position on the hillside: the dark mass of Big Wood, close-fitting as a pelt on the upper sweep of the hill behind the house, was the dense main force of the arboreal army. Clearly visible from almost any point in the surrounding landscape, the solid block of mellow brick supporting a blue-grey roof broken by five dormer windows and six great chimneys, conveyed an impression of strong endurance and pride, as well as a sort of fearless integrity, in its stark, ungarnished simplicity.

VII

BEHIND one of the seventeen large, polished windows of
Great Stone's imposing façade, an elderly woman with
grey hair and a shrewd, humorous face was sitting mend-
ing, with almost incredibly small stitches, a hole in a
white linen cloth. Her occupation and her plain, dark
dress gave an immediate clue to her position in the household, which was something between that of lady's maid,
companion, housekeeper, and poor relation. In order to
get as much of the afternoon light as possible, she had
drawn her chair close to the window, and her whole pose
suggested concentration upon her fine work. Yet it was
clear that her intent look was not for the sewing alone.
She appeared to be both waiting and listening for something. Though her needle did not pause in its regular
rise and fall, her eyes, during the brief operation of pulling
the thread taut after each stitch, frequently darted towards
the door, quick as minnows, behind their old-fashioned
spectacles. Her ears, too, must have been equally alert,
to have caught, as they did, the sound of approaching
footsteps several seconds before the daughter of the
house, whose governess she had been years before,
hurriedly entered the room.

Isabel Bonham was several years older than her brother
and could no longer, strictly speaking, be called a young
girl. Like all the Bonhams, she was tall and well-pro-
portioned, with light brown hair that fell naturally into
pleasing waves, regular features, and a rather charming
expression; these were her assets. She had none of
Anthony's striking good looks, but was a young woman

of amiable appearance, inclined to plumpness, and possessing a pair of singularly steady and pellucid grey eyes which seemed to be the indication of an honest, serene and unselfish nature. Just now, the gentle, reposeful expression that was habitual to her had been replaced by a look of perplexed anxiety. The hasty way in which she came into the room, pulling the door shut behind her, also indicated some unaccustomed mental disturbance.

The governess was the first to speak, carefully inserting her needle in the white cloth which she then allowed to fall over her knees, where it hung, draping her spare lower limbs like a cassock.

'Well, have you seen her?' she asked in a calm voice that, like her physiognomy, suggested a fund of quiet humour as well as much practical understanding of life.

'Oh, yes, I've seen her; and she's not in the least like what I expected.'

Isabel Bonham was moving restlessly about the large, airy room, once her schoolroom, which was furnished with a queer miscellany of articles from the more important rooms of the house: comfortable, shabby arm-chairs; rugs, and cushions that had seen better days; ornaments and pictures of which the family had grown tired or for which no suitable place could be found. She stopped for a moment in front of the bookcase that still contained her battered old text books of history, arithmetic and geography, side by side with Dickens, Trollope and a few devotional books, bound copies of *Punch*, and an isolated poet or two. Then she moved on to the window and gazed absent-mindedly at the sky where the March sun was sinking in a stormy splendour of gold and jagged copper clouds.

The elder woman had been watching her peregrinations with tolerance and an amused twinkle behind her spectacles.

'Suppose you stop roaming about like a caged lion,' she now remarked, not unsympathetically, 'and tell me what she *is* like.'

Isabel laughed and came at once to stand by her side.

'You must think I'm silly, Ticey, to get so worked up — and certainly this Celia Bryant isn't half as bad as I'd imagined. You know, when Anthony first told us about her, that she was a widow whom he'd met on the boat, I couldn't help picturing her as a sort of adventuress, probably very made-up and dashing-looking — the sort of vampire-woman you read about who fascinates men and lures them on to do whatever she wants.'

'And she's not like that after all?'

'Not in the least — except that there is something rather fascinating about her in a queer way. Not that I see it myself . . . And yet I can feel that there is something . . . something that would attract men, I suppose. I can't explain it — '

Miss Ticehurst gave a one-sided smile and smoothed a crease out of the cloth on her knee.

'Do you realize, Isabel, that you still haven't told me anything very definite about her?'

'Well, Ticey, she's not exactly easy to describe. The first thing that struck me was how young she looked — much younger than I am — she can't possibly be more than twenty. It's hard to believe that she's got a baby. Really, if she had her hair down, she'd pass anywhere for a schoolgirl. She's got lovely hair, by the way; real bright gold. I don't think I've ever seen it before except in pictures. Apart from that she's not a bit pretty — pale, and rather sleepy-looking, if you know what I mean.

Looks as if she hadn't much go in her. She's so quiet — hardly has a word to say for herself — just sits or stands about as if she were an image or something. You'd think from that that she was just a nonentity, but I'm afraid she isn't. There's something very positive about her, somehow.'

There was a pause while the governess sat still, contemplating the mental picture this description evoked.

'And how does Anthony behave now that he's got her here?' she inquired finally.

'Oh, Anthony — that's just what worries me so . . . He simply doesn't see anybody else while she's near him. When I went out of the room just now he never even noticed me going.'

A profoundly troubled look clouded the tranquil face of the speaker. Miss Ticehurst reached out and patted her hand.

'Don't look so unhappy, my dear,' she said, with unmistakable affection in her dry tones. 'Things aren't as bad as you think, I'm sure. It's just an infatuation. He'll get over it. I believe having her here is the best possible thing. You know how obstinate all the Bonham men are: if he thinks no one's opposing him he's not half so likely to do anything rash.'

'If only father won't try to persuade him to give her up — that would be fatal. And father's so impatient; he won't ever leave things to work out by themselves.'

Isabel was twisting between her fingers a thread of cotton which she had picked up from the arm of the chair. Occasionally she broke off a short piece of it. Before her companion could answer she went on:

'I'd so looked forward to having Anthony home again — it's been dull without him all the time he's been away on this trip. And now this has happened . . . I feel frightened, Ticey . . . That girl frightens me, I don't know why.'

'You're making everything seem worse than it really is,' the governess said comfortingly. 'He'll find that she's out of place in his own home, and he'll change his mind about her, mark my words.'

Isabel looked through the window again. The sun had set and the colour had gone out of the clouds, leaving them black and threatening. Dusk was rising up like smoke from the low lands. The ranks of fir trees lower down the slope bent their heads together and murmured lugubriously in the evening wind. She shivered and turned her back on the scene.

'I must go now. I ought to make sure that she's got everything she wants in her room.'

Miss Ticehurst again extended her hand. Isabel squeezed it gently, smiled at her and went out of the room.

VIII

CELIA had been at Great Stone for several days. She was sitting at lunch in the long dining-room with the three Bonhams and Miss Ticehurst who generally took her meals with the family if no important guests were present. Celia had finished. She folded her napkin automatically and then unfolded it again. It still did not come naturally to her to crumple the square of linen carelessly on to the table or let it fall to the floor as the others did at the end of each meal. It still seemed somewhat strange to her to have two men waiting at table. In the East she had grown accustomed to households of many servants, but they had been natives, quite different from this solemn butler and his grenadier-like assistant.

Sir Charles Bonham, a handsome, florid-faced man of about sixty-five, with white, wavy hair, sat at the head of the table in front of a portrait of his grandfather which — except for the fact that the painted gentleman wore side-whiskers — might have been a likeness of himself.

'Anthony,' he said, pushing his empty plate a little aside, 'I wish you'd do something for me this afternoon. Those people at Shimwells are complaining about their well; it seems that the sides are crumbling or something of that kind. I sent old Eb down to look at it, but he says that that well wasn't the work of his family in the first place, and he either can't or won't do anything. Ride over there for me, like a good fellow, and find out exactly what the trouble is, will you?'

The son — handsome like his father, for the good looks

in this family seemed to run all on the masculine side —
looked slightly taken aback.

'Well, Father, I'd go, of course; only as it happens I've
promised to take Celia on the links this afternoon. Can't
Coggin get over to Shimwells?'

Straightening the lapels of the check jacket he wore
over his yellow waistcoat, Sir Charles continued in the
same casual, friendly tone that he had previously used:

'Coggin's got to be up in Big Wood by three o'clock
to meet the woodman about those beeches that are coming
down. I shall be up there with them too. I'd be really
grateful if you could manage Shimwells — something
ought to be done right away. I'm sure Mrs. Bryant' —
the impressive, ancestral-looking head gave an embryonic
bow, the narrow lips smiled in Celia's direction — 'will
excuse you for once.'

The logs on the fire were making a hissing like rain.
But through the tall windows with their spotless panes
could be seen the lawns, the tops of the rare, bluish fir
trees below, the plain in the distance, all dusted over
with powdery March sunshine.

Celia felt resentment and distrust in her heart:
without looking at anyone she murmured formal words
of agreement and then became silent. She suddenly felt
suspicious of the amiable-sounding phrases which still
seemed to hover over the table, of the white curls framing
the old gentleman's ruddy face, of the governess's
observant glances, and of Isabel Bonham's gentle expression. She found that she was looking with enmity at
the fine, warm room with its Sheraton furniture and at the
table covered with good china and glass. In spite of the
gracious appearance of things, the atmosphere of the room
seemed to be dangerous to her. Only her lover was

without duplicity, smiling at her intimately as usual between the bowls of flowers that came fresh every day from the greenhouses. The young man was aware of no undercurrents of feeling. He was at home; what should he suspect?

'Well, then, if you're sure you don't mind, Celia, we'll put off the golf for to-day,' he was saying. 'We can practise those iron shots to-morrow morning.'

'All right.'

She smiled back at him, trying to reassure herself because he so obviously suspected nothing. Still, she felt very strongly that some hostile intention was in the air. Conscientiously she endeavoured to banish these thoughts, so inappropriate to the opulent room and its highly civilized occupants. 'After all, they're his people — he knows them far better than I do. He'd be bound to feel it if they were planning anything against me.'

'Perhaps you will walk up to Big Wood with me?' said the baronet almost cordially. 'I'm afraid my company is a poor substitute for Tony's, but there's a fine view from the top of the hill, and I can show you a grove of old yews that's worth seeing.'

THE gardens at Great Stone were all at the back of the house. In front there was only the great stretch of turf, like a giant's carpet of unbelievable size and thickness. Behind were the flower-beds, the terraces, the orchards. Most of the borders were still empty, but the apple orchard, full of newly opened daffodils, was a charming country picture — a springtime idyll. Higher up the hill larches were already green like emerald spears. The afternoon light was misty gold as if dusted with the pollen of innumerable catkins. A purplish bloom veiled the beechwoods. The air was sharp. Sir Charles Bonham and Celia walked up the hill together, treading on the grass that felt springy with life renewed.

As they went, Sir Charles kept up a flow of agreeable talk. In his easy, charming manner he drew his companion's attention to the arrangement of the gardens, house and outbuildings now spread like a map below them. He pointed out Little Stone, the ivy-covered house near the church where Coggin the agent lived and which formed the boundary of the property on that side. He spoke of different trees, whence they had come, when and by whom they had been planted. He did not seem to expect any special response from the girl beside him. His conversation was entertaining and almost a monologue; he spoke always of Great Stone and its environs.

They came finally to a crescent-shaped grassy space dividing the cultivated land from the woods. Above, between the grass and the beechwoods, stood the black ranks of immemorial yews. Mysterious whispers emanated from the funereal grove where archers, centuries dead, had come to cut their bows. Far below, the plain faded mistily into the horizon. The house, buildings, gardens, fields and plantations of Great Stone could all be clearly but diminutively seen, like a child's toys spread out on a carpet.

Sir Charles suddenly stopped walking and Celia also stood still. It was very quiet. Only the capricious sound of the wind was there, and the tiny voice of a boy shouting to scare the rooks far down in the distant fields.

'Of course, it's only a small place — a miniature estate,' the old man was saying; 'but I flatter myself that it's as near perfect as may be. The Bonhams have always loved their land; it means something very special to us. Tony feels just the same about it as I do, although it's not the fashion nowadays to mention such things as feelings.'

He shot Celia a keen glance. What was the best way of tackling the girl? There she stood, saying nothing, and staring out into space with those queer blank eyes of hers which seemed to be looking into another dimension. It was only a trick, a mannerism, she had of not focusing her eyes on any particular object; but it could be oddly disconcerting. It made one wonder if she were really paying any attention at all to what was going on round her: almost as if one were talking to a deaf person or to someone not quite 'all there'.

'Naturally, all this will belong to Tony one day,' he brought out; 'and to his children after him.'

She turned her head slowly, as if in remote surprise at this last unnecessary remark.

'Yes, of course. So I supposed.'

Sir Charles felt indignant and at the same time uncertain as to his own tactics. The cool way she answered, as though she hadn't much opinion of him! He had planned this walk and brought Celia up here with a definite object; but now he could not decide on the best method of achieving his purpose.

He had sent his son East on a tour of the company's main branches because such a tour was part of the Bonham tradition. It was supposed to broaden the outlook of a young man, to give him a glimpse of the world before he settled down to devote himself to Great Stone. But in Anthony's case it had led to that most undesirable eventuality — an 'entanglement'. When the boy had first mentioned Celia Bryant and suggested bringing her to the house, the father's heart had been filled with angry dismay, but he had raised no objection because he, like the two women of his household, realized the risk that lay in thwarting the obstinate Bonham male. 'A board-ship flirtation — nothing serious about it,' he had told himself. 'Let him see as much of her as he likes and get her out of his system.'

But the appearance of Celia had upset his calculations. He had prepared himself for a woman of the world, for someone scheming, or vulgar, or mercenary, or for the traditional 'merry widow' — for any sort of person, indeed, except the girl who actually arrived on the scene, so unexpected in her youth and her cheap clothes. 'What the devil does he see in her?' was the question constantly in the baronet's mind. That pale-faced, silent type was not much to his taste. All the same, there was no getting away from the fact that the two of them really did seem to be in love. Since Celia Bryant had been in the house, Anthony had had eyes for nobody else; and the girl, too, seemed to go about in a dream from which no one but Tony could wake her. It was specially galling to Sir Charles, who had always been first with his son, to find himself passed over for this insignificant chit. If only the girl had been beautiful or witty or fascinating in any obvious way, he could have borne the situation more easily. As it was, he felt that he had been wounded in his pride as well as in his affections.

During the time that Celia had been at Great Stone, he had done everything possible unobtrusively to win his son from her. But without success. Anthony had failed to respond to his advances. The old bond between them was no longer of first importance. Yet the father never doubted that the bond was still there, that it would still hold in a crisis. The claims of Great Stone and of the blood must win in the last resort; so it appeared to him.

And now he was determined to precipitate a crisis. He had put up long enough with this rival in his house, defrauding him of his son's love. She must go. That was why he had brought her up to this grassy place overlooking his demesne. In some obscure way he wished the lands and buildings which he also loved to witness her discomfiture.

But how best to open the attack? Once more he glanced at Celia's partly averted face. She wore no hat, and a strand of brilliant hair was blowing loose on her cheek, a feather of burning gold in the sun. She put up a leisurely hand and tucked the strand into place. The man's irritation mounted. Devil take it! How did one tackle a girl like this who gave no sort of a lead, but stood there dumb, with a look that seemed to say she thought nobody any great shakes? What was going on behind that colourless mask? Did money count for anything with her? Or the prospect of the title? — Or what?

Sir Charles's considerable stores of diplomacy and experience suddenly seemed useless. An out-and-out adventuress would have been far easier to handle.

'I'm getting an old man now,' he said, 'and my greatest wish is to see Anthony happily married and founding a family to inherit Great Stone when we are all dead and gone.'

'You don't consider me a suitable wife for him.'

Sir Charles was displeased by this remark. It was like the girl to express herself so crudely; no subtlety or finesse. He took out his gold case and deliberately lit a cigarette, sheltering the small flame of the lighter with his cupped hands.

'Ah, I see that you are in favour of outspokenness,' he said, speaking more urbanely than usual as was his habit whenever he was put out. 'And that being so I won't mince matters either. You are a very charming young lady and it has been a great pleasure to me to meet you. But, to speak frankly, I have other views about my son's future. Don't think me unsympathetic; I can quite understand how it all happened — tropical moonlight at sea — romantic atmosphere — the most natural thing in the world for Tony to lose his head and his heart. But now that you know his home, you must see for yourself,' his voice became smoother still, 'that a more appropriate match could be arranged for him among the families whom we have known all our lives . . . Someone with the same tastes and traditions as his own who would have the welfare of the estate at heart . . . Perhaps somebody with property adjacent to ours . . . Someone, at any rate, if you will forgive me for calling a spade a spade, of the same social standing, and without . . . er . . . encumbrances.'

'Anthony happens not to agree with you.'

Sir Charles inhaled the smoke of his cigarette.

'You're very sure of Anthony's feelings, aren't you?'

Celia felt a little cold. It was chilly standing up there on the hillside. Unconsciously she turned and stared at her companion. He was not looking at her but at the house down below.

'Are you implying that Anthony's feelings towards me have . . . altered?'

The baronet threw away his cigarette, stamped it into the turf with his heel, and, abandoning his suave manner, adopted a much more direct tone.

'I suggest that you should give him the opportunity of changing his mind should he desire to do so,' he said, suddenly looking her full in the face. 'My son is a chivalrous young man, and your presence here puts him in an unfair position. It is impossible for him to be certain of his own sentiments towards you when he is constantly in your company. I suggest that you allow him the freedom of coming to a decision uninfluenced by your nearness.'

'You want me to go away?'

'If you really have Tony's welfare at heart you will go. Don't you realize that, apart from any other consideration, your presence here is causing a lot of harmful gossip about him? Everything gets known in the country about people like us. All the scandalmongers in the district are saying by now that you, with your husband barely cold in his grave, have deserted your child to pursue Anthony and to force yourself into his home.'

'All right — I'll go — at once,' Celia answered, she hardly knew how or why.

Sir Charles was again all urbanity.

'There's no immediate hurry, you know . . . Don't put yourself out . . . I hope you'll forgive me for having spoken so bluntly, but it's no good beating about the bush, is it?'

He took off his hat in courteous farewell, and walked on to meet two men who were approaching from the direction of the wood. Celia stood still, then hurried down through the orchard by the way they had come.

IT was late in the afternoon before Sir Charles had finished his business with the woodman. He then walked to the agent's house, went into one or two minor matters, and drank a cup of tea with him before returning to Great Stone. When he had taken off his muddy boots he went into his study. He had done a good afternoon's work. He would sit by the fire for an hour and look at *The Field* and the daily papers before it was time to change for dinner. But first he must write a letter to the man who was buying his timber and make an appointment with him to look at the trees.

He sat down at his desk and took a sheet of the stiff, expensive notepaper from an embossed morocco case. The room smelt of leather and burning logs, long claret-coloured curtains shut out the doleful dusk, the air was warm and drowsy in the light of the lamps with their parchment shades. He had not had time to write many words when his son opened the door.

'Come along in, Tony,' he said. 'Did you find out what was the trouble at Shimwells?'

Anthony Bonham did not answer this question but came and stood close to the desk. A small, angry pulse was beating near the angle of his jaw and his nose had a pinched look that made him look older and more like his father than usual.

'What have you been saying to Celia, Father? When I got back I found her upstairs packing. From what she tells me you practically ordered her out of the house.'

Sir Charles put down his pen and straightened himself

in the heavy brocaded chair with its gilt arms, preparing for the struggle to come.

'I gave no orders,' he replied smoothly, 'but I certainly suggested that it would be advisable for her to terminate her visit shortly.'

'How could you be so inhospitable — so abominably discourteous to a guest? It was monstrous of you to do such a thing!'

The father stood up.

'Listen, Anthony! You must be reasonable about this affair! We can't keep the girl here indefinitely — everyone's gossiping as it is. Do you realize that the husband's only been dead two months, poor devil? It's positively indecent . . . We're getting ourselves talked about in the most undesirable way. Let her go home now — I'm not asking you to give her up altogether. Only don't see her for a time. Stay here and think things over quietly for a month or so, and then, if you still feel the same about her, we'll have to see what can be done.'

He tried to put his hand on his son's shoulder, but the young man drew back out of reach, and he was obliged to abandon the gesture with a sigh.

'Can't you see that all I want is your welfare, my boy?'

'I see that you've insulted the woman I love — turned her out as if you were dismissing a servant.' Anthony's voice was low and slightly muffled with anger. 'I demand that you should apologize to her immediately and invite her to stay on — if she will be sufficiently magnanimous to do so after such an affront.'

Sir Charles stiffened and his expression changed. He had not expected this. A cold flame of rage suddenly leaped in his heart.

'You know perfectly well that I shall do no such thing. You must be out of your senses even to think of it.'

He rested his hands on the desk, looked steadily into his son's angry eyes, and said in the frozen voice in which he was accustomed to give orders to unsatisfactory workpeople:

'This woman must go.'

'Then I shall go with her.'

The two handsome faces, so alike except for the dissimilar colouring of the thick, wavy hair with which each was surmounted, confronted each other in the implacable obstinacy of their common stock.

'If you leave Great Stone with her it will be for good. Do you understand me? You will not return here while I am alive.'

'Very well. If that is your ultimatum I accept it. Goodbye, Father.'

The short, brusque phrases sounded strangely in the warm, comfortable room with its shaded lights. The spoken words did not seem to bear any relation to their surroundings, but sounded incongruous as though a play were being acted between the four lofty walls hung with portraits and hunting trophies. The young man stood quite still for a moment, rigid, as if at attention, with clenched hands, staring back at his father who made no sign until with stiff, narrow lips he whispered in a tone of command:

'Go.'

When Anthony had left the room and closed the door after him, Sir Charles sat down again at his desk. He was trembling slightly. 'He chose that pale faced girl rather than me! Tony! Can it be possible that he has renounced me . . . his own father . . .? Well, he's made his choice and

I've done with him. I'll put him out of my life from this day on.'

All the same, he could not quite believe in what had happened. He had always felt so certain that in the last resort nothing could come between him and his son. The shock was too sudden. A few minutes ago he had come into the study feeling just as he always did, and now his life was a ruin. It could not have happened so quickly. The same logs were still burning on the hearth, the lamps still diffused their calm, honey-coloured glow. To associate tragedy with this familiar room was grotesque. 'No . . . No,' he muttered unconsciously; and again, 'No — '

Resting his chin on his hand he stared at a stuffed head on the wall with curious curling horns. The heavy horns were like the volutes of an Ionic column. The beast's face was narrow and its eyes reflected the firelight. Profound, mournful reproach was expressed in the dead animal face. Suddenly the reality of what had taken place came home to him, together with a sense of irrevocableness. His stubborn pride hardened to a core of pure opposition. 'Yes, very well . . . my son is dead to me.' Then another thought came into his mind — Great Stone. 'There will be no one to work for now,' he thought with a kind of barren despair. In the secluded study tears dimmed the old man's eyes for an instant. The house, the trees, the estate — without Anthony all these things which he had thought so dear to him now seemed of small account.

He recovered himself sharply as his daughter came into the room. He sat rigid in his chair.

'Father, what has happened? Why is Anthony going away so suddenly?'

She ran up to him, and stood leaning towards him across the desk. Her cheeks were pale with anxiety, her lips

parted and moist, and there was a look of fear and helplessness in her eyes.

'Have you quarrelled with him about . . . her?'

Sir Charles placed his hands on the carved arms of the
chair. His face was a stony mask which he had clamped
over his pain.

'Anthony is leaving Great Stone for good. He has
chosen that it should be so. In future you will not speak
to me of your brother.'

'Oh, Father! You can't do this . . . You can't mean it!
Only wait a little . . . Don't let him go to-night . . . all on
the spur of the moment — while you are both angry —'

Isabel was speaking breathlessly, almost weeping, incoherent with grief. A mixture of horror, supplication
and despair appeared on her distraught countenance. In
extreme agitation she came nearer and seized one of her
father's hands. He firmly pushed her from him.

'Control yourself, Isabel. There is no more to be said.
Please leave me alone now. I have a letter to write for
this evening's post.'

There was such inflexible authority in his voice that the
daughter turned slowly and hopelessly away.

CELIA had gone to bed early, tired after many hours
spent out of doors in the strong mountain air.

It was high summer in the mountains and even at night
time the air was warm. When she had undressed in the
plain, spotless bedroom of the small hotel, Celia went out
on to the balcony. It was like stepping into a world submerged in dark blue water. There was a fine view from
the balcony of the steep fields, the woods, the valley and
the mountains towering gigantic on every side. Now all
this was obliterated by the indigo darkness. Only the
mountain masses retained their primeval outline against a
sky 'sown with stars as a meadow is sown with flowers'.

The night had its own magic — a beauty more difficult
than that of the day. Only by slow degrees, and then only
partially, was the nocturnal beauty perceptible to blunt
human senses. The second hay crop had just been cut in
the sloping meadow below the hotel. A delicious, fresh,
summery smell breathed into the air from the cut grass
stems. On the bushes under the balcony the roses showed
faintly luminous, ethereal like hovering moths.

Celia leaned on the wooden rail of the balcony which
did not strike cold to her arms but seemed to retain, as if
reminiscently, a ghost of the warmth of the departed sun.
She looked up at the moonless sky where the constella-
tions pricked out their mysterious patterns. She gazed for
so long that the world and the mountains vanished and
there was left only the broken sapphire bowl of the sky
whose jagged rim followed the line of the mountain peaks.
As the minutes passed, the night slowly wove her into its

spell, holding her as if enchanted, without movement or thought.

Like noises heard in a dream there presently reached her the sound of someone approaching and entering the room behind her and of a man's voice calling her name with suppressed urgency.

'Celia! Celia! Where are you?'

Several seconds went by before she was able to recall her consciousness from the strange, deep blue ocean of oblivion which seemed to have engulfed it as it had also swallowed up rocks, trees, chalets, men and animals and all daytime detail.

'I'm here — out on the balcony.'

Anthony Bonham came through the long windows and, putting his arm round her, pressed her close to him. She could feel the hard cage of ribs under his clothing and flesh.

'When I came into the room and didn't see you I thought I'd lost you — I couldn't think where you'd got to. You mustn't frighten me like that. It's queer, but when I'm away from you, even if it's only for a few minutes, I have the craziest feeling that you may have vanished . . . that something may have snatched you away from me for ever.'

'Foolish Anthony; nothing could ever make me go away from you.'

Still half dreaming, she looked up at him. His face was indistinct, but some obscure emanation of excitement, of unusual repressed emotion, communicated itself to her, brought her back quickly to earth, and impelled her to ask:

'Where have you been all this time? It must be ages since I came up to bed.'

'I wanted to have a look at the English papers. They hadn't come before we started this morning, you know. Things are looking terribly serious — it means war, I'm afraid. The whole village is buzzing with rumours to-night.'

'War . . .' The short, sinister word sounded strange to her. She repeated it meditatively, savouring the strangeness, then pressed herself closer to him. Like a keen wind from the distant snows a breath of uncomprehended danger had suddenly risen out of the blue, sweet-scented summer night.

'It won't affect us, will it? England won't have to fight?'

'I don't know. It looks to me as if we may be forced into it. Anyway, I'm afraid it means the end of our time here. We shall have to go back to England — in case — '

'Go back to England . . . ? Do you mean soon . . . immediately?'

She stared into his face. In the dark she could see his eyes only like two black holes gazing back into hers. She suddenly began to tremble as if the night had turned cold. He bent down and kissed her, stroking her hair tenderly.

'You know I don't want to end our wonderful time. It's damnable that this should have happened.'

Celia clung to him tightly.

'Must it really end, Anthony? It's been so heavenly here with you . . . like living in a dream on the tops of the mountains. I don't want to go down into the world again. The world's waiting to take our happiness away . . . I hate England,' she added vehemently, 'it's always so cold there.'

'In midsummer?' he smiled gently.

'I don't want to go back. I want to stay in our dream for ever.'

A full moon had for the last few minutes been climbing up behind the jagged peaks on the left. Now it swung clear, and sailed triumphantly into the open sky, quenching the stars. The contours of the mountains were revealed, their buttresses streaked with ghostly ribbons of snow, towards which struggled blackly the ranks of the forest firs. The pastures below were glazed over with phosphorescent light. Unseen cattle were moving there. The faint clash of the cowbells floated up in the stillness, a mere spectre of sound.

Anthony did not answer.

'We mustn't be stranded here,' he said slowly. 'Supposing war is declared we might not be able to get away. If England does come in I shall have to be on the spot so that I can enlist at once.'

'You . . . would go and fight? But why, Anthony? What do you want to fight for? Why can't we stay here . . . out of it all . . .? What's it got to do with us? You're happy with me, aren't you? You said yourself that if we stopped here we wouldn't be able to get away — '

'You know we couldn't do that, Celia. We wouldn't be happy, either of us, that way. I'd always feel I ought to be fighting — not because of patriotism exactly, or any abstract idea, but for Great Stone. The old place means a hell of a lot to me — I suppose it's in my blood, somehow. And when I join up perhaps it will end the quarrel between father and me.'

'Great Stone . . . Your father . . . they're still more important to you than I am — more important than our happiness together.'

There was no bitterness in Celia's voice, but only sadness and a dreamy sort of surprise. While her husband had been speaking a strange sensation had crept over her.

It seemed as if life, which for a little while had forgotten them and left them in peace, had suddenly remembered to count its victims. A cold, baleful influence seemed to be reaching towards them, like fog rising up from the valley. To try to escape this evil influence or to fight against it would be as futile as struggling with the thick, clammy mist that sometimes enveloped the mountain village. 'It's the end, then; it's finished,' she thought heavily.

'I've never been really happy before,' she said as if thinking aloud; 'but now, whatever happens, I'll have this happiness to remember. Nothing can take that away from me.'

He held her closer again.

'Don't talk so sadly — as if everything were over — we've still got lots of happiness ahead of us. Perhaps there won't be any war, after all; it may be only a scare. There've been plenty of war scares before that have come to nothing. You know how much I love you, Celia. It's for your sake, too, that I want to put things straight with father. I'm proud of you, and I want you to be accepted properly as my wife. I'm not going to take the initiative, though. He was in the wrong, he insulted you, and the first move must come from him. But I do want everything to be put right — You and I established at Great Stone, and presently, perhaps, a son to inherit it all after us.'

'A son . . . You want me to have a child?'

'Why, yes, Celia; of course I do. There must be someone to carry on when we're gone.'

Although he could not see her face, the young man was struck by the tense, almost gasping sound of her voice when she answered:

'No, no, Anthony! Don't ask that of me . . . please . . .
I could never — '

He kissed her face and her hair, resting his cheek
against hers.

'All right. We won't talk about it if you'd rather not —
there's lots of time for that, anyway.'

His caresses soothed her and the acuteness of her
distress disappeared. As always, when she was in his arms,
she felt somehow transported; a wave of painful tender-
ness swept over her. Anthony stroked her hair softly and
in silence.

'I hate the thought of leaving this place where we've
been so happy,' she said. 'But if you want to go back to
England I suppose we must go,' She sighed. 'It doesn't
really matter where we are as long as we're together. I'm
happy just to be with you. But now I feel very frightened.'
She suddenly clutched his coat in both hands and gripped
him passionately. The ominous, cold shadow of future
events had fallen across her heart. A miserable vision
came to her of their two selves and all poor human
creatures as helpless children overshadowed by a black,
inexorable doom. 'I'm so frightened, Anthony . . . that
we may be parted.'

Anthony Bonham was still rhythmically stroking her
hair. Now and then he bent forward and pressed his face
into the soft mass that had the same fresh scent as that
which rose from the hayfield near by. Suddenly he became motionless. He could not find any words of comfort. He too was conscious of the threatening future, as of
a dark room, a room containing he knew not what, a room
which he was compelled to enter but from which there
appeared to be no exit.

The moon had risen up into the zenith. It looked small

and hard. A cold, unpropitious radiance now gave the roses under the balcony the meretricious appearance of paper flowers. The faces and hands of the lovers were blanched. In their pallor, their silence, their immobility, they might have been two young lovers overtaken by death in a last embrace. The profound tragedy of the universe oppressed both their hearts. Anthony was the first to make a difficult movement. Putting his hands on Celia's shoulders, he turned her towards their room.

'It's getting late,' he said. 'We must go inside. You'll catch cold if you stand out here any longer.'

THREE

THE war did not have much effect on the invalid's world of Marion Henzell. Being outside the current of life, she was also outside the current of destruction. Battles and the death-struggle of nations two hundred miles away were to her rumours fabulous and remote as news of a famine in China or a disaster on the other side of the world — things about which one read in the newspapers; deplorable, but quite without personal poignancy. Jessington was not in the line of air raids. No wandering zeppelin ever strayed that way to bring home the message of carnage with a casual bomb. Of course, the ration cards were rather a nuisance; the housekeeping was complicated to some extent by them and by the scarcity of certain food-stuffs. But the frugal Desborough House *ménage*, always accustomed to pinching and scraping, suffered little inconvenience.

Mrs. Henzell, with her tiny appetite, certainly did not experience any hardship. As long as she could keep up a good fire in one room and drink her weak tea several times a day she was content.

Now, on this cold January afternoon of nineteen-seventeen, she was sitting in the study, thinking agreeably of the tea which Mattie would be bringing at any moment. Her pleasure in this simple anticipation was only slightly diluted by the prospect of the arrival of her daughter later in the evening.

Celia and her parents were nominally on good terms; terms, that is to say, of conventional politeness on both sides. The prospective title had done much to reconcile the Henzells to her indecorously hasty re-marriage.

Ever since she started her war work in London more than two years ago, Celia had been in the habit of coming to Jessington every month or so to see little Clare. The girl usually travelled down from London on a Saturday by a train that arrived just after six o'clock. Clare would be in bed by the time her mother reached the house, and Celia would do no more that evening than look in at her through the door of the old nursery. Most of the next day she would spend with the child, returning to town in the late afternoon by the slow Sunday train in order to be at her desk in the War Office early on Monday morning.

This particular Saturday had been settled upon for her visit some time ago, before the news of Anthony Bonham's death. The sight of the young man's name in the casualty list had been the first real intrusion of the war into Mrs. Henzell's existence. But even that had not touched her closely. How could she be expected to mourn the death of a son-in-law whom she had never seen? The only way in which the matter affected her personally was with regard to Clare. She hoped that Celia would not now decide to take her away. The grandmother had grown used to having the baby girl and her nurse in the house. The money which Celia paid for their keep came in useful for the housekeeping. The nurse, a cheerful young woman always full of Jessington gossip, afforded a sort of light relief to old Mattie who was sometimes glum and cantankerous. Marion Henzell had wondered whether her daughter would postpone coming to Desborough House. But yesterday a note had arrived saying that she intended to come down as had been arranged.

The door opened and Mattie carried in the welcome tray which she placed on a small rosewood table beside her mistress's chair.

'Thank you, Mattie. You might put some more coal on the fire while you're here; it's bitterly cold this afternoon. You haven't forgotten that Miss Celia will be coming, have you?'

'No, I've not forgotten. Her room's ready for her. Though I'm surprised at her going about so soon after the bad news, I must say.'

Mrs. Henzell had already poured out a cup of tea, and the sight of the steam rising from the straw-coloured fluid made her feel charitable.

'I don't agree with you, Mattie. I think it's quite natural that she should turn to the child in her sorrow. And to think that now she will never be Lady Bonham after all ... How dreadfully sad it all is — '

The old servant grunted censoriously as, with the long, awkwardly shaped tongs, she lifted a heavy lump of coal and dropped it on to the red-hot fire.

'I always knew *that* marriage would come to a bad end,' she said. Her ancient joints cracked when she replaced the tongs with a clatter and stood up straight. 'Bonham begins with a B and so does Bryant — "Change the name and not the letter, to have died would have been better".'

'How can you be so superstitious!' the other exclaimed. 'All the same,' she went on, speaking over the rim of the cup from which she had just taken a sip, 'it does almost seem ... I mean to say, to be twice a widow before she's twenty-three — '

The two old women who, through nearly lifelong association, regarded one another more as friends than as employer and employed, looked into one another's eyes for an instant. The same gleam of somewhat morbid interest was noticeable on both their faces.

'You know, Mattie, I wasn't a bit surprised to hear he'd been killed. Perhaps I oughtn't to say so, but in a way I'd been almost expecting it. There really does seem to be something unlucky about poor Celia ... I wonder if she'll come into any money now?'

Just at this moment the speaker was astonished to see her daughter entering the room. A wave of discomfort passed over her.

'Celia! Here already —'

She put down her cup and rose in some confusion to greet the new-comer. The two met awkwardly in a perfunctory embrace as Mattie, muttering that she would fetch another cup, departed towards the kitchen.

'Yes, I caught the earlier train. We finished sooner than usual to-day.'

'I was so sorry to hear ... So terrible for you ... A hero's death ...' Marion Henzell was saying in her reedy, indefinite voice, fluttering her eyelids rapidly.

Celia deliberately, and as it were wearily, took off her coat, hat and gloves and came to the fire where she stood holding out her hands to the warmth. She was wearing the same dark clothes that she had worn all the winter. Her hair was cut short, her pale face and inexpressive blue eyes looked empty and exhausted.

'Don't let's talk about Anthony,' she said. 'Where's father?'

'He had to attend some meeting or other — something to do with the parcels for prisoners of war, I believe it was. Really, I don't know what things are coming to ... They must even have their meetings on Saturday afternoons now. Your father works far too hard — I scarcely see him for a moment these days. What with these committees as well as all his own work — '

Celia stood still. All the words that her mother was speaking passed over her like a flock of sparrows, leaving no trace. Her blank eyes were fixed on the fire.

Mattie brought in a clean cup and saucer, put it down on the tray, and left them alone once more.

'Will you have tea first . . . ? Or would you like to go straight up to the nursery? I expect Clare will be having her tea now.'

'I'll wait then, and go up afterwards,' Celia said.

She sat down by the fire and slowly began to drink the weak tea that was poured out for her. The feeling came over her, as it always did in this room, that she ought not to be there. It was her parents' sitting-room, the room which she had occupied so seldom during her life at Desborough House. The old sensations returned to her with the remembered stuffiness of the warm atmosphere. Nothing had changed. The canary hopped and chirped and scrabbled in its cage. Mrs. Henzell sat in the chair which looked as if it had been upholstered with a strip of brown carpet, and talked in her disconnected, indistinct, incoherent way, rarely finishing a sentence. The furniture was shabby and overcrowded. Everything looked drab. Although the room was clean, it seemed to have a stale smell of bird seed and dust.

Celia became aware that she was being asked a question. Her mother sat opposite, fidgeting among the tea-things with her small, wrinkled hands and glancing nervously at her with evasive eyes. Certain words caught her attention.

' . . . your plans about baby Clare — ?'

'There's no need to make any change,' Celia said. 'I

shall be able to go on paying nurse's wages just the same. With the pension and my own salary I shall manage quite well.'

'You mean to go on working at the War Office, then?'

'Yes, of course. I need the money. But even if I didn't I should still have to do something to get through the time.' She sighed, and a shadow passed over her face.

'Then you haven't . . . I mean . . . I thought, perhaps, that you might . . . have inherited something — ?'

Celia gave a short laugh that did not sound gay.

'Oh, no. I haven't come into a fortune, Mother. All Anthony ever had of his own was a small legacy an uncle left him when he came of age. We've been living on that capital ever since we got married and it's all gone now. His father never forgave him for marrying me. He never gave him a halfpenny after he left Stone.'

She stood up abruptly and put her cup and saucer back on the tray. All at once it seemed necessary to her to escape from the close room, immediately, regardless of what her mother might think, regardless of everything.

'I'm going to the nursery,' she said. 'Clare must have finished her tea by now.'

THE nurse went out with the tea-things on a tray and little Clare was left alone in the nursery. The room, like all the rooms of Desborough House with the exception of the study, was draughty and cold. The three-year-old child was hardened to the cold and did not notice it any more than she noticed the departure of the nurse. She sat on the floor, playing with an old toy. It was a box, painted pillar-box red, with slots of varying sizes and shapes in the lid into which fitted corresponding pieces of coloured wood. When the box had first been given to her, she had found it difficult to fit the right pieces of wood into their proper holes, but now her plump little fingers inserted them accurately and almost mechanically. To do this gave her a feeling of superiority, although it was really too easy to be amusing. She was a docile and sedate little girl, with rather old-fashioned, rather timid ways. She saw no other children, but lived contentedly enough in her restricted world. A strong east wind was rattling the windows. The draught under the door from time to time made the faded mat on the floor ripple like water.

The door opened and the window curtains blew out straight in the current of cold air. Someone had come into the room. It was not the nurse, but the bright-haired person whom Clare had been taught to call 'Mother'. The child felt no special interest in this visitor who appeared at what seemed to her immensely long intervals, was always quiet and distant, and did not seem to know how to play. She was also a little distrustful of her as an intruder from outside the nursery microcosm. She looked to see if the stranger had brought a present as she sometimes did, but there was no sign of one.

Celia bent down to her daughter and kissed her without warmth. Then she knelt on the floor and talked to her for a few moments. The pretty, serious child with her lint-coloured curls, responded with grave attention, her eyes wide and unmoved, her mouth a trifle uncertain. The mother rose and went across to the window where she stood, leaning against the sill, and gazing abstractedly into the room. Clare watched for a little to see if she were to receive any more attention; then impassively went on playing with the scarlet box.

Celia felt horribly tired. The loss of Anthony had filled her with a sense of utter exhaustion. His death had come to her not so much as a shock as like the climax of an interminable illness. She had never hoped that he would survive. A hundred times and on a hundred battlefields he had died to her since the war began. His death was a long-drawn torment that had started years before on a balcony, one summer night in the mountains. How long he had taken to die! It was almost a relief to know that it was finished at last. Yet how lost she felt now, how empty! People passed before her like phantoms, her mind was a blank. Work, forms to be filled in, words to be spoken, meaningless motions and sounds ... 'Nothing matters any more now'. The cold draught rippled the carpet like water.

'The wind in the trees makes a noise like galloping horses, like guns. Anthony died without seeing the trees he loved. If I had had a child perhaps his father would have forgiven him and he would have died happier. Why couldn't I do that for him?' The wind shouted, 'too late',

144

in the chimney; whispered, 'too late', in the ivy leaves outside the window.

Her eyes fell on the baby girl. 'Why is she here . . . and not Anthony's child? No one wants her — there's no sense in it.' Perhaps Clare too was a phantom and would disappear if she closed her eyes. No, when she opened them again the fair, curly head was still bending over the red box.

'It's only Anthony who has really vanished—whom I shall never see again — ' She clenched her hands in agonized protest. Tears burned at the back of her eyes.

Clare played with her pieces of coloured wood.

THE Armistice had been signed; the war was over; it was December. For the first time for four years an air of Christmas gaiety was starting to enliven the London streets. A few luxuries were slowly creeping back into the shop windows. This year there would be more food on the Christmas tables, more toys in the stockings of the children who had escaped the guns and the gas and the bombs. The children ran and slid on the frosty pavements, pressed their noses to windows full of toys or of cakes and sweets made with chemical food substitutes. They were the children who had escaped the war and would provide material for the next. Their time was coming.

Celia walked along the afternoon streets swept by a cold north wind, looking for the office of the lawyer whose letter was folded inside her bag. The traffic roared like surf on some glacial shore, people scurried with set, frozen faces, a race of northern ghosts locked in the icy cañons of the streets. A sense of abysmal futility overcame her as she hurried along. Anthony was dead. The war was finished. In a few weeks now, at the most, her work would come to an end. And then what?

Although she was only twenty-four, everything seemed to be finished. She had never been able to recover from Anthony's death. It was as if, when Anthony died, some small but important cog in the machine called Celia Bonham had slipped out of position. It was not a vital cog, because the machine continued to function after a fashion; but it functioned imperfectly. She was able to eat and sleep and work as before; she travelled in buses and trains, sat in cinemas, theatres and restaurants, carried on conversations in her usual rather vague, rather distant way. But a kind of sterility hung over everything that she did; inside, she was empty and lost. Nothing seemed to have any meaning. Her life was a senseless gibbering of phantoms.

Because of the indefinable charm of her bright hair and her pale, unresponsive face, men were attracted to her. They were intrigued by her strange, far-off manner that was both dreamy and cold, so different from the sexy vivaciousness to which they were accustomed. But Celia was not interested in them. She was indifferent to their attentions. She went out with them when they asked her for an evening's amusement. She was conscientiously appreciative up to a point. Altogether, she presented a fairly normal appearance to the world. But her heart was buried with Anthony, in the past. She lived, as it were, a life dedicated to his memory. Sometimes she wondered a little at her depression, at the unhealing nature of her wound. 'Why do I go on feeling like this? How can I still mind so much?' But the thought that she was young and healthy and that some day she might love somebody else never occurred to her.

The end of the war came as rather a shock. So long she seemed to have worked at her monotonous task, checking and filling and dispatching the endless flood of War Office forms, that she had somehow never envisaged an end. What should she do now? She had no prospects in view, no intimate friends. The thought of Desborough House lay like a cold stone at the back of her mind. Sometimes she had a fatalistic idea that the house was waiting for her; that she would be drawn back there against her will.

The letter which had come for her from the unknown lawyer had struck a faint spark of curiosity in her apathetic gloom. She had recently read in the paper the news of the death of Sir Charles Bonham. It meant nothing to her. He had lived well and had had a good time. Now he lay in the ground, the same as his son. Perhaps somewhere, in some mysterious way, they were reconciled. What could the lawyer want with her, writing and asking her to come and see him?

She had now reached the address that had been printed at the top of the letter. She paused, and then went inside the building.

THE man of business received Celia at once although she was a little early for her appointment. She had the impression that he had been awaiting the interview with some interest. He was a man of about fifty-five, bald-headed, with a vast, bulging, shiny forehead which overhung his face and gave him the appearance of a tremendously magnified embryo. When he had greeted her and installed her in a large leather arm-chair near his desk, he began at once:

'You are aware, I presume, of the death of Sir Charles Bonham?'

'Yes, I read about it in the paper.'

'You will not be surprised to hear that he left all his property to his daughter, Miss Isabel Bonham, who is his sole heir.'

Celia nodded without speaking. She felt mystified and detached at the same time. After the cold clamour of the windswept streets, the comfortably appointed office seemed full of a drowsy seclusion. She moved her gloved hand back and forward on the smooth, slippery arm of the chair and gazed at the lawyer's protuberant forehead.

He, for his part, was attentively eyeing the pale, quiet young woman who looked thin in his massive arm-chair. Celia's clothes were old but in good taste and she wore her hat with an air. Nevertheless, she did not give the effect of paying great attention to her appearance. It was obvious that she had not spent much money on herself. 'Probably hasn't got much to spend,' he reflected. He thought she looked tired and unwell. There was a lack of vitality about her that was hard to explain unless it were the result of physical debility.

'But perhaps it may surprise you to hear that Sir Charles was by no means a rich man when he died.'

'Really? I always thought that the Bonhams were a wealthy family.'

'They were until quite recently. Unfortunately, the war hit them hard as it did so many people with foreign interests. Sir Charles most ill-advisedly attempted to preserve the balance by speculation. He insisted, against all advice, in making several risky investments which resulted in the loss of a large portion of his capital. I need not go into details. The regrettable position now is that Miss Bonham inherits practically nothing except the estate itself. I hope to salvage enough to bring her in a trifling income, but it will be necessary for Great Stone to be let or sold.'

There was a pause. The lawyer was twisting a silver pencil between his fingers. He gazed at it pensively under his domed forehead.

'I really don't see what this has to do with me' — Celia glanced at the letter which had lain on her lap since the start of the interview — 'Mr. Rivington.'

The man set this remark aside with a wave of his pencil and proceeded to put a question:

'You paid a visit to Great Stone just before your marriage, did you not?'

'Yes; I stayed there for a few days.'

'During that time you became on friendly terms with Miss Bonham?'

Celia frowned slightly, trying to recall an image from the distant past. Before her mind there floated vaguely an imperfectly remembered form standing at an open door, a pair of eyes turning anxiously towards Anthony across a table banked with yellow spring flowers.

'No,' she replied slowly: 'I don't think we were exactly friendly, though she was kind to me as far as I can remember. I can't remember clearly at all. It's so long ago.'

'It appears to me that you have in Miss Bonham a very good friend indeed,' Mr. Rivington said rather sharply. Celia was not making a good impression upon him. He put down his pencil and looked straight at her. She returned his regard in silence. Her eyes looked empty and cold. 'What a peculiar expression,' thought the lawyer. He suddenly decided to come to the point.

'Miss Bonham was devoted to her father. As far as I know, there was during the whole of Sir Charles's lifetime only one difference of opinion between him and his daughter, and that was on account of his treatment of your late husband. Miss Bonham loved her brother very dearly. I think I am right in saying that only the strongest sense of filial loyalty prevented an open quarrel between her and Sir Charles at the time of your marriage to Mr. Anthony Bonham. At that time, and afterwards, right up to the day of her father's death, she continually interceded with him on her brother's behalf. Sir Charles, as you know, remained adamant to the end. He was a proud man, in some ways an obdurate man, and, rightly or wrongly, he was convinced that his son had acted unpardonably.'

Mr. Rivington paused and passed his hand reflectively over his bulbous forehead as he added:

'One must remember that all this time he — a man born and bred in the security of wealth — was being worried and embittered by financial losses.'

'Yes,' said Celia in a toneless voice.

The lawyer crossed his legs under the desk and leaned back in his chair, resting his elbows on the arms and interlacing his fingers.

'Miss Bonham feels that her brother suffered a wrong. It is not in her power, alas, to make restitution to him' — the eyes of the speaker were lowered for an instant and then focused once more on Celia's blank face — 'but in her generosity of heart she has conceived the idea of paying tribute to his memory — through you.' The last words were ejected like two pellets from between a pair of singularly straight, colourless lips.

Celia remained silent. The warm, enclosed room, the lawyer's voice speaking of people who seemed to belong to a past epoch of her existence, produced in her mind a curious effect of unreality, as though she were taking part in a fantasy, a scene which might have come from *Alice in Wonderland*.

'Although, as I have told you, Miss Bonham is herself in straitened circumstances, she has commissioned me to get in touch with you and to make a certain most generous proposal.'

'What is that?'

'She feels that reparation would be made for the past if she were to hand over to you a share of the small income which will be derived from the sale or letting of the estate.' Mr. Rivington coughed slightly. 'I think I should make it clear that I do not associate myself with this suggestion — in fact, in the best interests of my client, I felt obliged to advise her against taking such a course. However, she is set upon the idea . . . and you have only her disinterestedness to thank . . . if you care to take advantage of it.'

With an irritable movement the lawyer opened one of the drawers of the desk and handed Celia a paper.

'Here is the address; though doubtless you will remember it.'

'The address — ?'

'Miss Bonham's address, of course. The big house has been closed pending disposal, and she is living at Little Stone. You can get in touch with her there . . . That is to say, if you decide to avail yourself of her offer.'

His manner clearly indicated the conviction that, if she had any decent feelings at all, she would do no such thing. He closed the drawer with a decisive click and stood up.

Celia also rose, and putting the paper into her bag without looking at it, turned slowly away.

'I'll think it over.'

LITTLE STONE, where Coggin the agent had lived for a number of years, was a small, comfortable house covered in ivy. On one side was the church, in front was the village green from which the house was screened by a box hedge of such density that it almost resembled a wall. Between this box hedge and the house there was only a narrow strip of grass, for the garden was at the back. From the front door to the hand gate in the hedge ran a brick path, on one side of which grew a fine holly tree and on the other a very old yew clipped into a shape something like a gigantic acorn.

At the window of the room in which the agent had eaten his solitary meals, Isabel Bonham was standing with a duster in her hand. Coggin had departed and Little Stone was now her home. From this window, as from all the windows in the front of the house, Great Stone could be seen standing out boldly higher up the hill. It was a bright December day. The winter sun shone out of a sky that was the pale blue of an old china plate. The holly berries showed glistening red. A few sparrows were fluttering round the tree. Hoar frost still sparkled in the shadows which the morning sun had not reached as yet. Isabel had aged during the last four years; her brown, wavy hair was lightly powdered with grey. She was plump, and at thirty-three had already acquired the aspect of an old maid. Her face still had a gentle expression; but worry and grief had imprinted upon it a look of permanent sadness. She rested her hand on the window sill, gazing out at her old home.

Miss Ticehurst came into the room. The governess had changed less than her old pupil, having crystallized, as it were, into the form which would remain more or less unaltered until her death.

'Why do you stand there brooding, Isabel? It's not good for you. You know, I think you're making a great mistake in deciding to go on living here. Why don't you move away to some quite new place where you can forget past unhappiness?'

'I could never live anywhere else, Ticey. Stone is my home.'

'I think you're making a mistake,' the other repeated, taking the duster out of Isabel's hand. 'What good does it do to be always brooding over things that are done with and weren't your fault anyway? You'll be making yourself ill if you go on like this.'

Isabel certainly did not look well; her full face that once had had pretty pink cheeks was now quite pale.

'As for this idea of helping Anthony's wife . . .' The governess dusted a pewter bowl on the mantelpiece with repressed violence — 'Well, I hope I'm not un-Christian myself, but I don't agree with it. It's Quixotic, Isabel!'

The younger woman made no reply, but with grey, resigned eyes continued to gaze out of the window.

'It's not as if the girl were penniless,' Miss Ticehurst continued indignantly. 'She has the pension as well as her parents and her own home to fall back upon. Probably she's in a far better position than you are, if the truth were known. It's sheer madness to think of giving up any of your income to her! Why don't you come to your senses before it's too late? I know things have gone too far as it is for you to back out entirely . . . I suppose you'll have to see her now that she's written. Give her some memento, if you like — one of Anthony's pictures or a piece of jewellery — and say that things are worse than you thought ... that you find you're not in a position, after all, to help her financially ... For heaven's sake be sensible! Be guided by Mr. Rivington's advice if you won't listen to me.'

Isabel turned round and a pale ray of sunlight touched her hair as she moved. She smiled at the governess. Her eyes were pure, soft, dove-like grey.

'It's no good, Ticey. My mind's made up, and nothing will alter it. When I see Celia I intend to offer her a hundred a year. We shall just be able to manage here without that now that Great Stone is let — I've worked it all out to the last penny.'

The other made a sound between a snort and a groan, exclaiming 'Bonham obstinacy!' with a kind of half-humorous despair, and flicking her duster viciously at an imaginary cobweb in the corner of the room. She knew that it was useless to say anything more.

THE December sun shone with equal brilliance when
Celia walked up the hill from the railway halt where the
local train had deposited her. It was about a mile to the
village. All the time, as she walked, she could see in front
of her, like a landmark, the isolated mass of Great Stone.
The brick looked a dusty rose colour in the winter sunshine. It gave her a strange sensation to be returning to
this place where nothing seemed to have changed. Somehow it was hard to believe that all these years the house
had been standing there, exactly as she and Anthony had
left it. The pain of her loss was sharpened, but at the
same time she felt an inexplicable excitement like pleasure.
'Anthony loved Stone, yet he had to die without seeing it
again, and I am the one who comes back here,' she reflected, walking beside the road on the grass which, crisp
with frost, made a faint crunching sound under her shoes.

At Little Stone she was surprised when the door was
opened by an oldish woman with a shrewd, wizened face;
she had forgotten the governess's existence. Miss Ticehurst showed her into the small drawing-room with an
air of reluctance and left her alone. The sharp brightness
outside was reflected in the neat little room. The window
was still sunny. Clean chintz covered the chairs; a portrait of Sir Charles Bonham hung on the wall, miniatures
of his wife and of Anthony and Isabel as children were
pinned to a strip of blue velvet over the mantelpiece,
there was a slight smell of beeswax.

Celia received a second surprise when Isabel Bonham
appeared. She had expected to see someone much younger

looking. It seemed strange that this plump, ageing woman whose hair was turning grey should be the sister of the man she had loved. Yet there was some likeness — something — in the eyes, the turn of the head ... His ghost seemed to draw near. 'Anthony, Anthony,' her heart lamented, 'You were so young, so beautifully young! How could you die! How could you leave me for ever! Your body was beautiful. Dear Anthony. Where are you? Why have you left me?'

Isabel seemed pleased to see her. With her sweet smile she came straight up to Celia, shook her hand warmly, and invited her to sit down near the fire.

'I'm so glad you've come,' she said with sincerity. 'All these years I've been so unhappy about Anthony. I want, if possible, to make some small amend — ' She went on to explain what she had in mind.

Celia did not make any immediate response to her suggestion. Instead she asked a few questions: Who had taken Great Stone? For how long was it let? Did Isabel find her changed circumstances very irksome? The other answered in a frank, simple way. There was a pause.

'And you ... are you thinking of living in London for good?'

'No ... I don't know. I've no reason for living anywhere.'

Isabel repeated that she wanted to help her. Celia had taken off her gloves and was looking down at them pensively, smoothing them on her lap. Suddenly she raised her blue eyes which had their curious unfocused expression.

'Let me come and stay here with you ... You look at me so kindly — like *he* used to ...' her voice shook slightly. 'I don't want money — I've got enough. I'll pay for my keep and something more besides. I only want somewhere to live, where it's peaceful . . . with someone friendly and kind. I was never happy at home . . . I can't go back there. And now my work in London is finished. I'm a bad person . . . no one likes me. But Anthony loved me — if I could have stayed with him he would have made me good. When I fell in love with him I felt different . . . He was good and kind to me as no one else ever has been. And your eyes are like his . . . You make me think of him —'

Isabel Bonham felt as though a wild bird, a seagull perhaps, had flown into the quiet room and was circling about her with strange, disturbing cries, wailing and beating its wings. The other seemed a shattered, lost creature beside her. Tears dimmed her compassionate eyes.

Suddenly Celia slipped out of her low chair, sank on to the floor near her and distractedly clasped one of her hands.

'Let me stay . . . for his sake! I know I've no right to ask you, but don't send me away!'

'All right . . . don't cry . . . You can stay here,' Isabel answered almost without knowing it. So violent, so elemental, was the impingement of this stormy emotion upon her own virginal nature, that she felt confused for an instant. It seemed to her at that moment natural and even inevitable that this request should have been made and that she should have granted it . . . as if it had to be so. 'It's Christmas time — we must all love one another,' she thought vaguely, stroking the bright, bowed head that rested against her knee.

Only when Celia grew calmer and lifted again those strange blank eyes to her face, she felt a pang of something like dread, remembering how, long ago, she had said, 'That girl frightens me — I don't know why.'

VII

CELIA sat by the drawing-room fire, writing in a thick book which she held on her knee. Although it was only five o'clock the curtains were drawn and the room lighted, for it was dark as midnight outside. Another Christmas had come and gone since her first journey to Little Stone. For just over a year she and her daughter had been members of that small feminine household, and now it seemed to her that she had never lived anywhere else. Some unanalysed instinct had urged her to bring the little girl whom Mrs. Henzell had wanted to keep at Desborough House. 'It will only be a short visit,' she had said to the grandmother. But she had dismissed the nurse at the same time, saying that she intended to look after Clare herself in future.

The generous and bereaved heart of Isabel Bonham had opened at once to receive the child. Suddenly uprooted from her nursery world, snatched away from all that was safely familiar, Clare's rather timid nature had suffered a shock which made her appear nervous and difficult. Small, diffident, helpless, with the terrible helplessness of the child who has no say in its own destiny but, like a dog, is utterly at the mercy of its owners, she had been brought to Little Stone. No one had consulted her wishes, no one given her any explanation of the change which had completely disorganized her existence. She did not struggle or complain, but accepted everything, as the child must always accept, being altogether in the power of others. But she had also the child's need to depend on someone, to attach herself to some particular person upon whose support she could rely. She did not know to whom to attach herself. In all her actions there was, besides the defensiveness of her apprehension, the touching eagerness to please, the eternal, pathetic anxiety of the unloved child.

Isabel Bonham saw this anxiety and her heart was wrung. A new and poignant emotion gripped her when she embraced Clare for the first time and felt the too-quick, too-eager pressure of the clinging arms round her neck. Something that had frozen within her since the deaths of her father and brother stirred painfully to returning warmth. With sure instinct the child sensed her response and clung to her from the beginning. Day by day she grew dearer to the lonely woman, until Isabel began to dread the time when Celia would speak of departure.

How fortunate it was that things should have turned out like this, Celia thought, sitting alone by the warm fire.

She had not wanted to leave Little Stone. It suited her very well. She had felt at home here from the start. All the same, had it not been for Clare, she doubted whether Isabel would have invited her to share the house permanently.

Soon after her arrival she had started writing again. The manuscript of her first unfinished novel had long since been destroyed, and she had never until now felt the urge to begin another. But once she began to work, she wrote fluently and with enjoyment. The peaceful, almost slumberous atmosphere of the village was perfectly suited to concentration, as was the simple, orderly, smooth-running house of women in which she lived. Isabel, Miss Ticehurst and Rose the daily servant between them took her six-year-old daughter almost entirely off her hands. The novel was finished in the summer and published a few months later. Although it had not brought in much money, it had been rather more than mildly successful. The reviewers were uniformly encouraging. Now she had recently started work on a new book, the opening chapters of which seemed to be shaping well.

Having come to the end of a paragraph, she closed her book, got up, and put it away in a drawer of the walnut desk near the window. The imaginary characters which, like so many eidola, had occupied her attention until now, slowly faded out of her mind, making way for reality, long exiled by their fantasmal shapes. She moved the curtain a little and looked out. The unlighted village green was sunk in mid-winter darkness. The night was raw, a strong south-west wind was blowing.

Presently she dropped the curtain and turned back into the room which seemed to have grown cold during the last few minutes. The fire had died down, and she threw a log on to the red embers, standing in front of the fireplace to warm her hands. Her eyes rested automatically on the miniature of her dead husband. The painted boy's face gave her a familiar feeling, half wonder, half pain. 'His bones are in France, but that isn't he any more than that picture. Where is he?' She could not bring herself to believe that he had passed completely out of existence. Her love rejected her mind's acceptance of annihilation.

Suddenly the noise of a car made itself heard above the rushing sound of the wind. 'That must be Dr. Turner,' she thought. For over a week now the doctor had been coming each day, sometimes twice a day, to visit Miss Ticehurst who was seriously ill in her bedroom upstairs.

There had been an epidemic of influenza in Stone.

Isabel Bonham had been the first of their household to succumb. She had gone out one cold afternoon to see an old woman in the village. She still kept up an interest in the people who had formerly been tenants of the Bonham family, visiting them from time to time and helping them in a modest way when they were in need. On her way home she had suddenly started to shiver and her legs had begun to ache horribly. In the house she still could not get warm, but sat shivering and aching until she was persuaded to go to bed. Her attack had not been a serious one, however, and she was soon about again, though not before Clare had caught the infection from her. Clare's attack had also been slight, but the governess, who had nursed them both, was severely stricken. During the last few days her illness had taken a still more serious turn, and there was even some doubt as to her ultimate recovery. A hospital nurse had been installed in the house, as Isabel, weak from her own convalescence, was unequal to the strain of constant nursing, and Celia had not offered to undertake it.

'I wonder if she's going to die,' Celia reflected, listening to the doctor's footsteps as they mounted the stairs. She would not be sorry to have Miss Ticehurst out of the way. She knew that the ex-governess distrusted her and disliked the ascendancy which she had almost unconsciously obtained over the sweet-natured Isabel. There had never been anything more cordial than a state of armed neutrality between the elderly woman and herself. 'She's never approved of my living here; she'd like Isabel to turn me out of the house.'

VIII

In a moment or two Celia left the room and went upstairs. It was cold on the landing, but she paused outside
the door of the sick-room. An unnatural portentousness
seemed to emanate from the closed door. Subdued noises
were audible inside the room. A glass tinkled, there was
a murmur of voices, the nurse's footsteps tapped briskly
about. The listener stirred uneasily. The sort of shudder
passed over her which makes people say, 'A goose is
walking over my grave'. The sounds which she heard
seemed to recall to her some memory from the far distant
past, a memory that would not take definite shape, but
which left upon her mind a confused, distressing, ill-
omened impression.

Her disagreeable feelings did not at once disappear
when she went into her daughter's room. The little girl
was losing her babyish prettiness. Her hair had darkened
although it was still very fair; it was now no longer the
colour of lint but of straw, and instead of curling it hung
in a loose, heavy wave, turning in at the ends. Her complexion was pale, and her eyes, sometimes blue, sometimes
grey, sometimes almost green, often looked empty as
glass, just as her mother's did. There was a striking resemblance between them. Feeling limp after her illness,
Clare was now curled up listlessly in an arm-chair, doing
nothing at all. A picture book was open on her lap, but
she was not looking at it. When Celia opened the door
she glanced up hopefully, then, seeing that it was not
Isabel who entered, animation died out of her face.

In her uneasy mood, Celia felt the indifferent, uninterested look go right through her. The child's face seemed particularly blank, and her pose, in its undisguised, languid boredom, struck her as especially irritating. Celia looked coldly at her. She felt cross and resentful. She thought of Desborough House and clearly pictured to herself the bleak nursery with the draught blowing under the door, the worn-out rug rippling like water ... Clare ought to be grateful to her for taking her away from that dreariness and bringing her to this cheerful, warm room.

'Why are you sitting there doing nothing?' she asked. 'You've got plenty of toys to play with.' She frowned. It seemed an imposition that she should be bound in any way to this dull, unresponsive child.

'I don't want to play,' Clare answered in a flat tone. Celia shrugged her shoulders impatiently, turned her back on her daughter, and began in an absent-minded way fitting together the pieces of a jigsaw puzzle that was spread out on the table. There was a silence in which could be heard the muffled noises of the doctor's departure.

After a while Isabel Bonham came into the room. Her expression, the shadows under her eyes, the way her steps seemed to falter, all indicated weariness and grief. Celia disturbed the pieces of the puzzle with an abrupt movement and turned round to ask:

'Well, what did the doctor say?'

'He says there's no hope. He doesn't expect her to live through the night.'

These words made an odd effect on Celia's mind. She was glad to think that she would be rid of her enemy and yet at the same time she felt troubled, as if something unlucky had happened. Muttering conventional sympathy, she went away, leaving the other two alone together.

As soon as the door had closed, Clare jumped up from her chair and threw her arms round Isabel's neck. The childish embrace broke through the elder's reserve and a few tears fell silently on to the thick, fair, heavy hair. How lonely Isabel felt now! The blow which was about to fall would deprive her of her last support, her last link with the dear past. Her home, her fortune, her father, her brother, all, all were gone, and fate could not even spare this one old friend to console her bitter loss. The fire-light danced heartlessly through the tears on her eyelashes.

'Don't cry . . . dear Isabel! I love you — ' Clare was whispering in her ear.

Her arms clasped the small figure with feverish hunger. 'Clare . . . Clare . . . You're all I have left now — ' Two more tears slipped into the fair hair like raindrops losing themselves in the long grass.

It was summer, and Clare Bryant was happy. In the midst of the world which seemed so vast and dangerous to her, so full of change and precariousness, she had found one enduring rock to which her thin arms could cling. Isabel Bonham would not alter towards her or leave her alone. Isabel had promised that, whatever happened, nothing should separate them, no one should take Clare away from Stone. The child felt implicit confidence in the grey-haired woman from whose clear eyes nothing but kindliness and honesty looked out. The anxiety lifted from her young heart. At last she had a place in the world. Little Stone was her home.

Living as she did a rather solitary existence with play-fellows few and far between, her interest turned towards non-human things. Clare loved the changing seasons, the slow-moving cycle of the year filled her with endless excitement. The appearance of the first dangling hazel catkins brought her a message of private joy at the end of the winter. Now she envisaged the earth as a woman trying on dresses in reckless haste, no sooner arrayed in one than she cast it aside to put on another. The dresses of early spring were simple and crisp as organdie — fresh greens and all shades of yellow, Japanese patterns of pale blossoms spotted on blackish stems. In a few brief days, so it seemed, spendthrift nature discarded these virginal garments for more flowery ones, chaste sprays of blossom gave place to the luxuriant patterning of greenery, summer was fully installed.

This afternoon Clare was going with Isabel to fetch

some raspberries for jam making. There were no raspberry canes in the garden of Little Stone, but the Phillimores had promised to supply Miss Bonham with several pounds from the gardens of the big house which had once been her home. Although they seldom met, Isabel was on quite friendly terms with these tenants who had taken Great Stone on a long lease.

Clare was in her happiest mood as she walked along carrying the basket lined with a cabbage leaf which was to hold the fruit. This was just the sort of expedition that she enjoyed most. She was always trying to coax Isabel to talk about the mansion which could be clearly seen from all the front windows of their own house. To the little girl it seemed a romantic, fabulous and altogether enchanting place, made even more enthralling by its associations with her beloved friend. She could imagine no greater delight than exploring those mysterious gardens, and perhaps even obtaining a glimpse of the interior of the house itself.

It was a hot, sunny day. A light wind was stirring a silvery leafed tree like a shoal of minnows, the leaves of the beeches hung arrested in their upward green rush. The footpath to Great Stone skirted the churchyard. Clare's eager eyes searched among the gravestones for a certain tree, a golden cypress of some rare species, the clipped fronds of which curled softly as the tips of ostrich feathers. How lovely it was! Her sandalled feet made dancing steps on the dusty path. She looked up at the deep blue sky across which small white clouds were moving serenely, like choir boys in procession, from west to east. Then her gaze turned to Isabel who was walking quietly beside her, looking with soft, sad eyes towards the house on the hill.

'You'll take me with you, won't you, when you go back to live at Great Stone?'

'What makes you think I shall ever go back there?'

Clare had run to the edge of the path to examine a butterfly that had just alighted on a clump of scabious. Against the faded mauve of the frilled flower the small blue butterfly showed clear as a jewel, with white thread-like lines on its delicately pulsating wings.

'Oh — the banished prince always gets his kingdom back in the end, doesn't he?' she said, stooping over the butterfly. In her mind she was seeing Isabel as the heroine of one of her fairy tales. The butterfly flew away and she ran after her companion who was now a few paces ahead.

'Yes, you shall come with me if I ever go back.'

'And we'll live there always — just the two of us — and be happy ever after?'

'Yes, Clare,' answered Isabel, with her sweet, melancholic smile.

Satisfied with this promise, the little girl walked on in silence for a while, swinging her basket, and watching the birds, the insects, the flowers, all of which she looked upon as her friends. Suddenly her quick eyes caught a different, larger movement than those of the sub-human world. The two of them had by now climbed a good way up the hill towards the great brick house standing alone under the dark tree line which followed roughly the shape of an inverted U. One of the points of the wood was actually slightly below them, and it was in the shadow of these outpost beech trees, skirted by the bridle path from Owlswick to Stone, that Clare had detected the sudden glint of metal catching the sun.

'Look, Isabel! Isn't that Mr. Temple riding down there?'

169

The woman turned, shading her eyes with her hand. At the edge of the wood, a good field's breadth away, a figure could now be clearly seen, mounted on a tall bay horse. The handsome, long-legged animal, dappled with alternate sunshine and shade, was walking over the rough ground, stepping high and setting its feet down with fastidious grace.

All at once the rider saw the two people higher up on the open slope and waved his hat in greeting. Isabel and Clare waved back to him. The three trivial gestures faded out and were lost in the immensity of the hot afternoon, insignificant as the salutations of ants under the enormous blue sky across which clouds like seraphs marched in complacent order.

In the villages of Owlswick and Stone, Francis Temple was considered rather a mysterious man. According to the village way of thinking he was still quite a stranger in the district, for it was only a year or so before the war that he had moved into the Grange at Owlswick. He had no connections in the county, nobody knew who he was, where he came from, or why he had chosen to live in the obscure village that was divided from Stone only by the wind-swept shoulder of Callow Down. The explanation of the last point was simple. Both he and his wife had wanted a country home not too far from London; in the course of a tour they happened to come upon the Grange standing empty, liked the look of it, and, being by that time thoroughly tired of house agents and house hunting, purchased it there and then.

Once installed, they began to lead the usual life of wealthy people in the country, to ride, and play games, and entertain. It was clear that they had plenty of money. But this state of affairs did not last long. The war came. Francis Temple, who at an earlier period of his life had held a commission in the regular army and was on the reserve of officers, rejoined his unit immediately. Later on he took out a draft to reinforce a garrison in Egypt where, with short intervals of leave, he remained until the Armistice.

It was typical of the whole life of this fortunate man that he managed to get through the war in a way that brought him credit, and yet at the same time was not only virtually without danger, but even quite agreeable to him.

His wife did not stay at Owlswick to await his return. Shortly after her husband's departure she left the village and the Grange was shut up. It remained closed for several years. The Temples were thought to have left the neighbourhood for good. Then, in the early spring of nineteen-nineteen, everyone was astonished to hear that preparations were being made to reopen the house. Francis Temple reappeared on the scene, but this time without his wife. It was vaguely rumoured that they had parted, that the marriage had not turned out a success. Mr. Temple set up a modest kind of bachelor establishment at the Grange, leaving most of the rooms closed, employing only a housekeeper and one or two servants, keeping one thoroughbred horse in the rambling stables. He used the house mainly at week ends, though in fine weather he would sometimes spend a week or more consecutively in the country. Nobody knew how he occupied the rest of his time. He was understood to own a flat in London.

In the old days there had always been gaiety, visitors, luxury at the Grange. Now all this was changed. People said that Francis Temple must have lost money during the war. The truth was that he himself had never possessed anything more than a quite moderate income; it was his wife who was a wealthy woman. Now that they had separated it was all Francis could do to maintain his *pied-à-terre* in London as well as his week-end quarters at Owlswick.

He was a man of somewhat extravagant ways. He had always been accustomed to dress well, to eat and drink expensively and to ride good horses. He had to have these things. Life below a certain standard of luxury was inconceivable to him. He was always considerably in debt, but this did not disturb his optimistic, light-hearted and rather irresponsible nature.

He had allowed himself to drop out of the social life of the district, partly because he could no longer afford to entertain, but mainly because he was bored by the conventional country people. In any case, he spent so little time at Owlswick that he did not want to be bothered with dull callers. It was his habit to describe himself as a man of simple tastes, and though this seemed contradictory, in one sense it was not untrue. He was perfectly content with his horse, his water-colours, his car and his garden. Nevertheless, his equable care-free manner, his elegant appearance and his gay smile predisposed people in his favour, and he was generally given a cheerful greeting when he rode by on his fine bay horse.

He had become acquainted with the Bonham family in the days of his pre-war affluence, and Little Stone was one of the few houses which he still visited. He was always welcome in the small feminine household. The two women who lived so quietly and so out of the world were entertained by his conversation. Clare found him an amusing companion; Rose, the maid from the village, thought him a romantic figure and was always delighted to cook pancakes for him if he stayed for a meal. He was essentially a man who was popular with women.

To-day, having waved his hat to Isabel and Clare on the hill, he rode on down to Stone in a rather pensive mood. He was glad to think that he would find Celia alone.

CELIA did not find it necessary always to sit at a desk when she worked at her novel. She was not the sort of writer who sits down to the manuscript in a business-like manner at certain fixed hours with a dictionary and a thesaurus at hand. On the contrary, she liked to write at odd times and in odd places, generally with the thick exercise book held on her knee.

This afternoon, when her daughter and Isabel had set out for Great Stone, she took a cushion and sat down to work on the front door-step in the sun. It was a favourite place of hers when the others were out of the house, sheltered and warm, and away from the noise of Rose at work in the kitchen. The high hedge concealed her from any rare passer-by; she liked the strong, spicy smell of the box in the hot sunshine.

Reality slowly retreated from her as her characters took shape, strengthened from flimsy ghosts into living figures, filling her consciousness with the peculiar patterns of their fate. In the hot stillness she sat absorbed. Words slowly crept along the lines until a page was filled.

Suddenly she looked up with a start, recalled abruptly from her private world of the creeping words. A man in the early forties, mounted on a tall bay horse, was looking at her from the other side of the gate in the massive hedge. He took off his hat, and his hair which was thick but quite grey on the temples, stirred in the warm wind. His face, with its large Roman nose and rather small chin, was tanned by the sun and distinguished by a cavalry

174

moustache several shades lighter than his dark brown hair; in the moustache, too, a few grey hairs could be seen. A pair of beautifully cut breeches and a light coat set off his slight, small-waisted figure; glistening chestnut-coloured boots displayed the admirable shape of his legs.

'I'm afraid I startled you,' he said with a smile.

'Francis! I didn't hear you coming — and I wasn't expecting to see you, either, so early in the week.'

'It seemed a shame to stay in town this lovely weather. I came down yesterday instead of waiting till Friday.'

Francis Temple sat watching her from his high horse. The animal shifted and tossed its head, there was a jingle of metal, the saddle creaked. 'She's in one of her queer moods,' he thought to himself. Celia was cut off from him in her unreal world; he could almost see a cloudy emanation surrounding her, through which he could not penetrate.

'I see I'm disturbing you at your work, so I'll be off now,' he said with his pleasant lightness, gathering up the reins and seeming to be on the point of turning the horse away from the gate.

Celia closed her book and stood up quickly. 'No, don't go.' She made an effort and banished the imaginary figures that had gained dominion over her consciousness. Glancing in the direction of the holly tree, she suddenly saw the spiked leaves like pieces of dark, shiny paper pasted on the blue afternoon. 'Come inside and talk to me. Isabel and Clare have gone out, but they'll be back soon and then we'll have tea,' she said to the man.

Francis Temple was pleased.

'Do you mean that? Are you sure you wouldn't rather I went away?' Receiving assurance that he was welcome, he dismounted, fastened the horse to the gate, and followed her indoors.

The drawing-room felt cool. Curtains had been drawn to shut out the strong sunshine which filtered rosily through the chintz, filling the room with a light like sunset water. In the vases and bowls there were many flowers from the midsummer garden — roses, carnations, blue delphinium spears.

'I'm rather glad to see you alone for a minute,' said Francis taking a small box from his pocket. 'I've brought you a little present from London. I hope you'll like it.'

Celia fingered the box which was made of black leather ornamented with a tiny gilt wreath. She felt curiously reluctant to open it. The idea came to her that once she had pressed the spring that lifted the lid, everything in the room and in her own life would suddenly become quite different, as if a powerful genie were imprisoned in the little case smelling of expensive leather. She was uncertain whether she wanted to release the genie or not. She glanced at her companion. He was watching her with rather an odd expression, stroking his moustache with his fore-finger, waiting for her to open the box. 'He's almost middle-aged,' she thought irrelevantly. She could not delay any longer. The spring emitted a faint click as she pressed it, the lid sprang back. On a bed of padded white satin a ring was revealed, a single, large, oval stone set simply in platinum.

'Francis! How beautiful! What a wonderful present!'

He was gratified by the effect his gift had produced, by the faint flush of rare animation it had brought to her pale face.

'The black opal reminded me of you, somehow. Put it on, Celia, and see how it looks on your hand.'

Celia's eyes had unconsciously turned to the miniature over the mantelpiece. 'Anthony has been dead a long time,' she thought, glancing down at the curious dark jewel, flashing with submerged fires. 'There's nothing left of him now ... except bones that might have belonged to anyone. I shouldn't recognize his bones.'

'Aren't you going to try it on?' Francis Temple was asking, with an expectant air.

She slipped the ring on to her third finger. How mysteriously it flashed there! The opal was like a dark, smoky cloud, pierced by changing flashes of deep red, orange, and emerald green. Sometimes a point of strange, sulphurous blue flickered in its depths. She looked up again at the miniature. 'Perhaps the shells smashed even his bones into powder. Perhaps there's nothing at all left of him ... Anthony, does any part of you still exist ... anywhere?' The painted boy's face gazed back at her, bright, heedless, unchanging, with half smiling lips. It seemed to her that at that moment Anthony was for the first time utterly lost to her. 'There's nothing ... he's gone — ' she thought confusedly to herself. Her thoughts were uncertain and vague.

'How nice it looks on your finger: and it fits perfectly.' Francis Temple came close to her — she had lowered her eyes from the miniature. He took hold of her hand and turned the ring slowly from side to side, making the stone flash.

'You have beautiful hands. You ought to wear lots of rings. If I were a rich man I'd like to buy you emeralds.' He suddenly lifted her hand and kissed it, then put his arms round her and held her close. 'Don't draw away from me. You know I love you, Celia. I've been in love with you for a long time.'

'Why has Anthony left me?' she thought. 'I know he's gone now . . . And who is this man holding me like this? Why am I here with him . . . what does it mean?'

All at once she let herself relax in his embrace.

'You're in love with me?' she repeated as if absent-mindedly. 'And you'd like to give me emeralds — '

The queer, light pricking of his moustache on her skin made her think of her father.

XII

FRANCIS TEMPLE, one of life's favourite children, had a knack of getting his own way without putting himself to much trouble. He was unexpectedly competent in small practical matters, and he had the gentleman's trick, the man of the world's trick, of making other people work willingly for his advantage.

As soon as he had seen the black opal on Celia's finger, he had made up his mind to spend the evening alone with her. He had put up his horse at the inn as he was accustomed to do when he stayed at Little Stone for a meal. Then he had gone into the village post office and telephoned to his man at Owlswick, a small, silent, swarthy person named Sands, who combined the duties of chauffeur, groom, valet and general handyman. As a result of the telephonic conversation, Sands had conveyed certain orders to the housekeeper before driving to Stone in his master's car which he left outside the inn while he rode the horse back over Callow Down, whistling quietly through his teeth all the way.

Francis had had tea with the ladies at Little Stone. He had been amiable and amusing as he generally was, had eaten several small seed cakes which Rose had baked specially for him, and had played a game of ball with Clare on the lawn at the back of the house. Then, when the little girl had gone to bed, he had coolly announced his intention of taking Celia to dine with him at Owlswick. He wished, he said, to ask her advice about some new chair covers.

Celia was not particularly surprised by the invitation,

although she had not been expecting it. It seemed quite natural to her to be sitting beside Francis in the light grey two-seater, driving through the summer landscape, where all was sweet-scented peace. The car was a Mercedes, smartly upholstered in bright red leather that matched the poppies shedding their frail, silky petals in the long grass at the roadside. Francis was a skilful if somewhat dashing driver. He often liked to drive fast and did not mind taking an occasional risk. But this evening he was in no hurry.

They drove at a leisurely pace along the road at the foot of the hill. The wind rustled the skirts of the beeches. The village dipped out of sight. But by turning her head slightly Celia could still see the solid block of Great Stone standing alone on the hillside. Presently the road curved round the point of the wood and the high trees hid the mansion from view. It was six miles to Owlswick by road — almost twice as far as it was by the bridle path.

Celia had never visited the Grange before. She was rather curious to see the abode of this mysterious individual who, for some unknown reason, wanted to make love to her and to present her with emeralds. Like Stone, the village of Owlswick was on the slope of a hill, but the Grange was lower down, beyond the village, on flat ground. Francis drove between wrought-iron gates, up a long drive bordered with trees where starlings settling down for the night were making a confused noise. The gardens were rather neglected; long grass, which someone had started to cut with a scythe, grew where there had once been a wide lawn. He pulled up in front of the big white house. Four of the upper windows were gabled with a small stone balustrade in front of each one. A heavy stone porch surmounted the front door by which they entered.

Francis Temple had accommodated himself to his reduced circumstances as simply and naturally as if to inhabit a large house, most of the rooms of which were shut up, were a perfectly usual procedure. His bedroom, his dining-room, and the small study where he spent most of his time with his books and painting materials, were always kept as immaculately as if he employed a large staff of servants. The dinner ordered by telephone was excellently cooked and served on a polished table decorated with white roses. The food and drink tasted no worse because the tradesmen who provided it had not been paid for a long time. After the meal was over and while it was still daylight, Francis showed Celia his paintings, slight, transparent-looking water-colours, displaying a fanciful talent. Then he proposed to show her some of the rooms that were not in use.

Celia accompanied her host along passages clotted with shadow. From time to time he would throw open a door, saying, 'This is the Tapestry Room', or 'the Blue Room', or 'the Long Room', and she would peer vaguely into some twilit apartment where the shapes of furniture shrouded in dust covers floated like dim, small icebergs, imponderable. The sight of all these uninhabited rooms had a strange effect upon her, not at all pleasant, though she could not have said why. When they entered the oblong drawing-room where for some reason or other the dust sheets had been removed, she was aware of a faint but definite sense of repulsion. It was growing too dark to see anything clearly. Some plaster pillars loomed like narrow ghosts, there was a sepulchral sheen of satin blanched of all colour. Celia fancied that the influence of the departed Mrs. Temple imbued the closed room with a sort of stagnant hostility.

She was glad when the tour of the Grange came to an end and they returned to the lighted study. It was a whim of Temple's to burn only candles, and the little room was full of a delicate, homely light. Here, in his own private room, the master of the house seemed to become much more real. He suddenly dropped the light, entertaining manner which he had used all through the evening, put his arm round her shoulders and kissed her gently on the cheek, saying:

'Come and sit on this sofa beside me.'

A tremor passed over her, a curious little flare of excitement ran over her nerves. Once again she was conscious of the feeling which she had experienced that afternoon in the drawing-room at Little Stone: the feeling that everything in the room, everything in the whole world, perhaps, had suddenly become quite different. She even felt as though she herself were not the same person who had woken up in bed that morning. Before, it had been the opening of the black jeweller's box that had initiated the change. Now it was Francis Temple, dressed in his beautifully tailored clothes, slight and elegant, with his smooth, experienced hands and his cavalry moustache, who seemed to have altered everything. She did not feel about him in the least as she had felt about Anthony Bonham. To her, Francis was still the almost middle-aged man who was fond of pancakes. Yet it was also he who, in spite of the unemphatic candlelight, revealed everything to her with a new freshness, as if she had emerged all at once from a long twilight. For more than two years, ever since Anthony's death, she had been living in half darkness. Now Francis had brought a light into that obscurity. The flowers, the furniture, the framed water-colours on the walls, the blue-hearted candle flames, all were swimming in this novel radiance.

Celia allowed herself to be drawn gently on to the sofa. Francis was speaking to her in a low, affectionate voice to which she did not pay much attention. She felt light and contented, almost disembodied, as if the Moselle they had drunk at dinner had made her slightly intoxicated. The soft sofa cushions supported her as buoyantly as a cloud. With a dream-like sensation of joy her eyes dwelt on the steadily burning candle flames, each one of which was surrounded by a tremulous, iridescent nimbus of light. It was as if she saw such flames for the first time in her life. 'How pretty they are,' she seemed to be thinking; and yet there were no definite thoughts or words in her mind. The bright, unwavering flames seemed to have passed into her very being. Francis had begun to breathe more rapidly than usual. She could feel his warm breath on her cheek, like a message to which she would have to listen sooner or later.

XIII

ISABEL BONHAM spent an unhappy evening alone. The
latter part of the day had altogether been full of painful
emotions for her. The visit to her old home had been an
experience not easy to bear with fortitude. The gardener
at Great Stone had worked for the Bonhams ever since he
was a lad of fourteen. Now he was getting an old man, still
hale and vigorous, but with grizzled hair and joints
knotted with rheumatism. As he filled her basket with the
pick of the raspberries, and while Clare rapturously
explored the nut walk and the sunk garden, he had talked
to Isabel about old times and about his new employer.
The Phillimores, it appeared, treated their people
generously and well. The head gardener's wages had
been raised at Midsummer. Nevertheless, the man would
have preferred to work for his old masters at a lower wage.
It didn't seem right, he declared, to have strangers living
in the big house. Great Stone belonged to the Bonhams,
and things would never seem as they ought until a Bonham
was installed there again.

Seeing Isabel's distress and thinking to comfort her, he
had gone on to show her how the gardens were being kept
up exactly as they had been in her father's time. 'Sir
Charles wouldn't find a ha'porth of difference anywhere,'
he said with some pride. But the familiar sights only
increased her bitter nostalgia for the place. Indeed she
would have found the situation more tolerable if there had
been drastic changes. It was all she could do to keep the
tears from her eyes as she looked at the house, mellow in
the afternoon sun, with gleaming windows behind each

one of which had been enacted some scene of the dear past; at the flower beds, the lawns, the trees, all with their precious associations. The same — and yet quite different: reft for ever of beloved presences; removed from her. 'I feel like a ghost must feel, haunting the earth long after its time,' she thought to herself.

Had it not been for Clare, she would have fled as soon as her basket was filled. But she had not the heart to cut short the little girl's enjoyment of the outing, although she herself suffered under the onslaught of eager, childish questions.

It was with a sense of achieving sanctuary that she passed through the gate in the tall box hedge when they returned to Little Stone. All the way down the hill she had been painfully conscious of the big brick house behind her which, although she could no longer see it, exercised upon her the effect of a vigilant eye boring into her back as she went along. She was glad to hurry indoors and shut out that eye.

But almost immediately she was assailed by a fresh disquietude. No sooner had they sat down to tea with their visitor than Isabel noticed the ring on Celia's finger. The younger woman had stretched out her hand for a piece of bread-and-butter, causing the opal to emit a spark of slow flame. Isabel's eye was held in a sort of fascination by the dark jewel, burning with sluggish fires, which looked like a strange beetle, a scarab, that had alighted on the otherwise ringless hand. The sight of it gave her a queer shock. Celia, she knew, possessed no jewellery. The ring was certainly new. It seemed obvious that Francis Temple must have given it to her. Yet neither of them mentioned it. The absence of comment, more than the actual gift, struck Isabel as being ominous and sinister, and she herself, inhibited by their silence, was unable to speak of it.

Although the behaviour of Francis was the same as usual, amiable and light-hearted, she could not get rid of the idea that there was something different about the man who was eating seed cakes with an appreciative expression, carefully brushing the crumbs from his moustache. When later on he carried Celia off to Owlswick to dine with him she knew that her vague fears were justified.

She ate her solitary supper without appetite. She felt restless, apprehensive, uneasy. Some fresh misfortune was threatening her unlucky life. She did not know yet what it was, but she felt its shadow upon her. After the meal had been cleared away she went upstairs to Clare who had suddenly cried out in her sleep, a thing most unusual for her. The child had had a bad dream and clung to her, trembling and tearful, begging her to promise that she would never leave her. Isabel gave her word and comforted her. When Clare was sleeping again she went back to the drawing-room. Before sitting down to read she stood at the open window and looked into the warm, glimmering night. She stared for a long time at the lighted windows of Great Stone. Again, as on two previous occasions, she felt frightened of Celia, without quite knowing why. A sensation of weakness came over her so that she almost stumbled into a chair.

Just before eleven o'clock she went upstairs to bed. The front door was unlocked, there was no need to sit up for Celia. But when she had undressed and lain down she did not feel sleepy. She lay awake for what seemed a very long time. The church clock struck twelve drowsy strokes. Owls hooted in the luminous summer dark. At last she heard the hum of an approaching car which halted outside. A conversation ensued, but the noise of the engine drowned the speakers, and she could not distinguish the man's voice from the woman's. Presently the car drove away and Celia entered the house alone. Isabel waited a minute, then put on her dressing-gown and went downstairs, impelled by an instinct which she did not examine.

Celia had gone into the drawing-room. When Isabel looked in at the open door she saw the other woman standing beside the desk, gazing dreamily down at the manuscript book which she had apparently just taken out of its drawer. Her rapt, impenetrable, dream-like expression sent a chill to the heart of the onlooker.

'Celia! Surely you're not going to start writing at this time of night?'

Celia turned round in remote surprise. Her blue eyes had an intent, rather inward look.

'No. I was going to take my book upstairs with me in case I feel like working early to-morrow morning. But why are you up so late?'

'I couldn't sleep. When I heard you come in I thought I'd come down and have a word with you.' She paused for a moment and then asked rather diffidently: 'What sort of an evening have you had at Francis's place?'

'Oh, quite pleasant ... he showed me all over the house.'

Isabel watched her attentively, apprehensively. Something in Celia's abstracted, indifferent manner filled her with inexpressible dread. Her heart began to beat very fast. Celia put the book under her arm and went on:

'We looked into all the rooms. I suppose he thought I should like to choose one for myself as I shall be going to stay there.'

'You . . . are going to stay . . . at Owlswick?'

'Yes. That is, unless you would prefer Francis to come here.'

She was not looking at Isabel but was searching for a pencil in the top drawer of the desk. Now she glanced up quickly in response to the tense, unnatural tone in which the next words were spoken.

'Francis Temple is in love with you . . . That's why he gave you the ring.'

'Quite right.'

Isabel took several steps forward, clenching her hands and breathing irregularly.

'And you've fallen for him, too. Celia, you stupid girl! Don't you know he can't possibly marry you? He's had affairs before, but his wife's a Catholic and won't divorce him — '

'I know all about that,' said Celia calmly. 'He's told me everything. And it doesn't make any difference.'

Isabel drew back, appalled. Her round cheeks became quite white and she started to tremble so violently that she could only speak spasmodically and with difficulty.

'You mean . . . you are going to live together . . . in sin . . .? You can say that . . . in this room . . . in front of Anthony's picture . . . in sight of Anthony's home — '

'Anthony has nothing to do with it,' Celia said in rather a callous tone. 'He's dead now — he's been dead a long time. Francis and I are still alive.'

The effect of these words was to shock Isabel into a state of temporary composure. She stopped shivering and stood absolutely rigid. The thought, 'She really is wicked, then,' passed through her mind. 'How right poor Ticey was in distrusting her. But Anthony loved her once. There must be some good in her — if only I

188

can appeal to it.' She found that though her mouth felt dry she could now speak quite normally.

'You can't do this thing, Celia. I implore you to have no more to do with Francis — to give him up immediately — never to see him again.'

'May I ask what right you have to interfere with my private life?' Celia inquired coldly.

'I am Anthony's sister ... I'm trying to protect his good name which you propose to dishonour. I'm not asking this for my own sake, but for his ... Don't you remember telling me how much you loved him? I've always believed it — that you did love him. Surely you can't have forgotten all that? Don't you realize how it would hurt him ... how ashamed he would be — '

Isabel's voice gradually sank lower and lower until it faltered away, silenced by the impervious attitude of her hearer.

Celia was not at all moved by this appeal. The words which the other woman spoke with such genuine emotion sounded foolishly sentimental to her. She felt tired, bored and detached all at the same time, and determined to bring the conversation to an end as quickly as possible.

'It's no use arguing with me,' she said, moving towards the door. 'I don't want to live in the past any longer. I'm entitled to do what I like with my own life, and I mean to go and live with Francis at Owlswick.'

'And Clare?'

'She will come with me, of course.'

Isabel made a spasmodic movement, coming between Celia and the door, barring her way.

'No ... no! You can't take her away from me — '

Celia stopped, standing still with the book under her arm, and gazed at her companion's convulsed features

Her own eyes were reflective and cool. She thought distastefully of the Grange with its many unoccupied rooms, its neglected garden running to seed. 'It would really be better to stay here,' she thought to herself. 'Francis wouldn't mind. He'd be comfortable and we'd save money. We'd have much more to spend on other things. And Isabel could go on looking after Clare. It really seems the most sensible way — '

'Then Francis must come here,' she said aloud. 'It could easily be managed. He could have Ticey's old room.'

'You suggest living here . . . under my roof, both of you . . . How can you be so shameless, so wicked?'

'Don't talk theatrically, Isabel. Anyone would think to hear you that this was the first time two people had ever lived together without being married. I assure you it's quite an ordinary arrangement these days. We're not living in Victorian times now, you know. If you want to keep Clare you can, by letting Francis come here. The decision's in your hands. You can please yourself.'

While she was speaking, Celia's eyes had automatically turned to the miniature which seemed to be watching her reproachfully from its narrow oval gilt frame. The bright boyish countenance now filled her with irritation. She put down her manuscript book on a chair and crossed the room to the fireplace. Leaning on the mantelpiece, she looked closely at the painted face that no longer meant anything to her except a source of annoyance. The eyes seemed to look back, directly, innocently and accusingly, into hers. She did not care. She felt impatient, changed, indifferent. Without a word she unfastened the miniature from the blue velvet and thrust it out of sight in a drawer of the desk.

Isabel hid her face in her hands with a strangled sob.

FOUR

It was the middle of March, about three o'clock. There had been a spell of unusually mild weather and the season was well advanced. The grass of the village green was already spangled with daisies and golden dandelions. The rooks were making a great to-do in the elm trees behind Little Stone, cawing and squabbling and flapping clumsily about their refurbished nests.

Clare and Isabel had been to the post office and were now walking home in the sunshine. The sedate, rather old-fashioned child had grown into a thin, quiet girl with a clear, pale face very like her mother's, and heavy, dull-yellow hair that turned in at the ends. Her eyes, more grey than blue, sometimes had the same peculiar unfocused look that was so often noticeable in Celia's eyes; but in the case of the daughter the calm, abstracted, inward expression was replaced by a dreaming look that, under the stresses of life, might easily turn later on into something much more abnormal.

Just now those grey-blue eyes with their somewhat disquieting possibilities, were seriously investigating the miniature jungle of grass stems in the churchyard bank, travelling a Lilliputian journey among the dry forest monsters of last year's growth and the already succulent green undergrowth, in search of the white violets which concealed themselves behind the dark scented shields of their own leaves.

Clare did not care what Celia did as long as she herself was left with Isabel, the one person whom she could trust. It made small difference to her that Francis Temple had come to live with them at Little Stone. The years which pass so quickly in later life seem infinitely long to a child, and she could now hardly remember a time when there had been no smiling, well-dressed intermittent visitor with a curled moustache in their household.

Francis had installed himself in the little ivy-covered house near the church as simply and unostentatiously as he had lived at the Grange. He was one of those happy people whose determination to take life easily seems to coerce circumstances into aiding and abetting their resolution. Anything unfavourable or antagonistic in his surroundings he simply contrived to ignore. He took absolutely no notice of Isabel Bonham's coldness, although she avoided him as far as possible, and, when forced into his society, treated him with a distant politeness that was the nearest approach to open hostility of which her gentle nature was capable. As if totally unaware of this, his conduct towards her remained, as it always had been, light, charming and friendly in a quite superficial way.

He was, as Celia had predicted, perfectly willing to transfer his person, his considerable amount of luggage, his man Sands, his horse, his car, his painting outfit, and a few valuable trifles, from Owlswick to Stone. By this arrangement he effected a great financial saving as well as relieving himself of all the troublesome business of housekeeping. The Grange and most of its contents had been sold, thus saving him a lot of expense and putting a useful lump sum into his bank account. The rooms at Little Stone, though small, were comfortable and furnished with sufficient taste to satisfy his rather high aesthetic standard. Isabel was a good manager and Rose an excellent cook. The little girl Clare was quiet and unobtrusive. Sands attended to all his personal wants. His horse was stabled at the inn near by, where a garage had also been found for his car.

Finding himself happily possessed of more money than he had owned for a long time, Francis was able to spend it in a manner most satisfactory to himself and to Celia. His old chambers in Jermyn Street had been replaced by a larger and more modern flat in which they spent a good deal of time, visiting theatres and the ballet, concerts and art galleries. They also travelled as much as they could afford, sometimes spending several months abroad.

This state of affairs was accepted by Clare as a matter of course. When she asked where her mother had gone and was told that she and her friend were in London, or Paris, or Cannes, or Vienna, she did not think it strange or make any further inquiries, but quietly continued the routine of her existence with Isabel. And when Celia and Francis returned, she accepted their reappearance unquestioningly, neither expecting nor receiving any account of their travels.

She was not actively aware, either, of the isolation of the house behind the thick box hedge. She knew nothing of the scandal that had originally been caused by Francis's taking up residence there. Now the scandal had died down, time had robbed the situation of its piquant appeal to the gossip-mongers, but the ostracism remained. There were a few people in the district, long-established friends of the Bonham family, who, for old times' sake, would have disregarded the conventions and visited Isabel. But she, with some trace of her father's pride, held herself sternly aloof, shut off from all social contact by reason of her acquiescence in Celia's guilt.

Most unjustly, it was Isabel who had to bear the heavy burden of disapproval: she alone suffered under the ban imposed by society. Neither Francis nor Celia cared that they had no friends at Stone. Laughingly, they congratulated themselves on having eluded the irksome attentions of dull country folk. They had acquaintances in London and in other places, their constant changes of scene took the place of social activities. When they came to Stone they were content to remain in seclusion, Francis riding and sketching and idling away the time, Celia busily writing, adding year by year to her modest literary reputation and to the short row of volumes bearing her name. Only on Isabel's friendly soul fell the weight of an unnatural and unmerited loneliness.

Clare had no inkling of the suffering of which she was the innocent cause. As far as she was concerned, the coming of Francis had brought few changes to Little Stone beyond the taciturn presence of Sands about the garden and house, and the sight of the grey Mercedes and afterwards of a newer and larger car, waiting — but not for her to ride in — outside the gate.

It certainly did occur to her sometimes, though in no urgent manner, that it would be nice to talk to someone of her own age. The Phillimores at Great Stone had two daughters, one slightly older and one a good deal younger than she was, of whom she caught glimpses from time to time about the village. These two little girls, the children of rich people, always smiling and prettily dressed, were objects of especial interest to her, and she had invented a private game, a sort of interminable serial story, in which they played leading parts. When, therefore, she saw them coming towards her along the path by the churchyard, she abandoned her search for violets and stood watching them with the unembarrassed scrutiny of the young.

The elder girl was talking to the governess by whose side she was walking, but the younger one, who was slightly ahead, paused beside Clare and returned her gaze with interest. Seeing the white violets in Clare's hand her eyes widened admiringly.

'Pretty flowers,' she said, stretching her hand towards them.

'You can have them if you like,' Clare answered. 'I can find plenty more on this bank.'

She held out the small bunch of violets, but before the other could take them, the governess hurried up and dragged her off by the arm with an angry look. Clare could hear her scolding the child as they walked quickly away. She suddenly felt sad. In some way the incident had wounded her.

'Why wouldn't the governess let her speak to me?' she asked Isabel. 'She wanted the violets and I should have liked to give them to her.'

Isabel did not reply to the question. She put her arm through Clare's, and they walked on, linked affectionately together, towards Little Stone. The face of the woman wore a look of preoccupation. Her eyes were harder than usual. Some difficult decision was achieving itself in her brain. Clare did not pick any more violets.

By the time that they reached the house, Isabel's purpose was fixed. She sent Clare into the kitchen to help Rose who was making scones for tea.

She herself paused for a moment in the hall. At once there settled upon her face the look of intense sorrow which she had refused to allow to be seen there during the girl's presence. Everything was quiet. Francis Temple was out somewhere, on horseback, or perhaps driving his car. He and Celia had arrived from London only a day or two earlier to enjoy the precocious spring weather. The cawing of unseen rooks came from the elm trees behind the house. Through the small window beside the front door Isabel could see the brick path, the gate in the hedge, the hillside, and part of the façade of Great Stone. The church was invisible to her, she could not see the peaceful graves or the cross beneath which her ancestors lay. Her face looked immolated in the shadowy hall. Shadows laid their grey wreath on her brow. She had a sensation of dreadful loneliness. No one saw her sacrifices, no one cared for her pain. Her fulfilment was in lonely suffering, and bereavement was her destiny. The Lord himself seemed to have hidden his face from her.

She took hold of the handle of the drawing-room door and turned it. 'When one has lost everything, life can't hurt one any more,' passed through her head.

Celia was sitting at the desk. Her manuscript book was open in front of her and she had a fountain pen in her hand. Her bright hair, much livelier, much more golden than Clare's, curled softly into the nape of her neck. She looked young, vital, attractive, assured. She did not turn round at once, but continued to bend over the page with an absorbed expression. Isabel studied her dispassionately, from a new detachment.

'There's something I must talk to you about,' she said. 'It would be a good time now as we're alone.'

'Not now — I'm working. I don't want to be interrupted.'

'Well, you'll have to be interrupted for once. I must speak to you.'

Isabel said this with rather an odd intonation as she came and stood near the desk. Her face still wore its sad expression, but added to this there was now something unusually positive, even forceful, that sat strangely upon its soft contours. The look of determination was the result of a cup of suffering filled to overflowing at last. She no longer had anything to fear from Celia: how could she ever have felt frightened of her?

'It's about Clare,' she went on in the same resolute tone.

Celia twisted her pen and then laid it down. Isabel kept her eyes fixed upon her. She wondered a little at this new-found courage that seemed to be putting words like cold pebbles into her mouth.

'Clare must go away from here — to school. She must be educated properly: I've taught her all I can now and she's quite old enough to go to a boarding school.'

Celia looked surprised and somewhat displeased.

'I thought you were so keen on keeping her here with you.'

A spasm passed over Isabel's face.

'Do you suppose it's easy for me to let her go? . . . the one human being left in the world who cares anything for me. No . . . But for her own sake she must go away . . . to lead a healthy, happy life with companions of her own age.'

'I don't see anything wrong with her present way of living.'

Celia looked down again at the half-written page in front of her, absenting herself from the talk. What on earth had come over Isabel, bursting into the room and wasting her time like this? It was a bore that she should have got this bee in her bonnet about Clare all at once. It would cost a lot of money to send the child to school; money for which so many more important and amusing uses could be found. It was certainly not an idea to encourage — a mere unnecessary expense. Celia's mind, which had not yet fully detached itself from its imaginary world, began once more to follow the written words. Suddenly Isabel bent forward and closed the book with a bang under her nose. An incongruous and almost ferocious gleam had appeared in her mild grey eyes.

'Don't think that I'm going to allow you to make her as unhappy as you've made me! You've done enough damage, Celia, in your time. Father and Anthony, who'd never had a quarrel in their lives before you came along, died estranged and miserable because of you. Anthony had to leave his home and the places he loved — because of you. You've spoilt my life too — made me into an outcast in the village where I've lived ever since I was born . . . I know you only too well by now. You're bad and unscrupulous and utterly selfish . . . You haven't the least grain of moral sense — '

'What has this interesting analysis of my character got to do with Clare going to school?'

Celia concealed her amazement at the other woman's

outburst behind an ironic voice and an expression even less legible than usual.

'I'm not going to stand aside and watch that child suffer for your sins,' Isabel answered more calmly. 'She's getting to an age now to realize things, and she mustn't grow up friendless and with an inferiority complex about being different from other young people.'

Celia made a movement of annoyance. There was silence for a few seconds.

'And supposing I decline to fall in with your ideas about my daughter's future?'

Isabel flared up again suddenly.

'Then you and Francis can leave this house immediately — yes, and take Clare with you! I'd rather never set eyes on her again than see her growing more warped and miserable every day. You've imposed on me long enough, Celia! I know you've only been making use of me from the start. Poor old Ticey was cleverer than I — she saw through you when you first came here. But I, like a fool, was taken in by your smooth face and your pathetic talk about loving Anthony. I might have known you were only acting, for your own ends.

'It's been convenient for you to have Little Stone as your headquarters — a place where you could live and write undisturbed, without the bother of housekeeping or the expense of an hotel. You traded in the most unprincipled way on my love for Clare to force me to countenance your immorality under my own roof ... You've never even pretended to care for your child — to take the slightest interest in her. It's suited you very well to have me take her off your hands and save you the wages of nurses and governesses.

'You seem to think that because you've got a talent for

writing you can do anything you like — that you're a privileged person. But I . . . when I think of what you've done to me and to the people I loved . . . I sometimes think you're almost a devil. You could never bring anything but unhappiness to anybody — except, perhaps, a person like Francis who's as amoral and heartless and calculating as you are yourself.'

Celia's eyes had gone unfocused and cold. She was a little disconcerted by this lengthy denunciation from a quarter so unexpected. Was she really guilty of all these things of which Isabel accused her — of being calculating, immoral and egoistic? Anyway, the elder woman seemed to have come to the end of her tirade. There was a pause. Celia examined the cover of her manuscript book. She fancied that it bore the imprint of Isabel's angry fingers. She looked up suddenly.

'All right. Clare shall go to school next term.'

For a little while after she was alone she sat still, staring straight in front of her. Gradually the defences which she had mobilized against the griefs and vexations of life, defences which had been temporarily scattered by Isabel's surprise attack, reassembled themselves and presently restored her to her usual impregnable position. Taking up her pen she began to write. All her doubts vanished in the absorbing, accommodating, unreal world where she spent so much of her time, escaping to the unassailable realms of her imagination.

Mrs. Henzell was sitting in the summer sunshine in
the garden of Desborough House. Her sparse, straggling
hair was now quite white, countless small, fretful lines
crossed and re-crossed each other on her face which, in
its thin, dry, bony bloodlessness, resembled the mask of
an old woman carved in ivory by some Asiatic craftsman.
It was Sunday, and she held on her lap, besides an un-
opened newspaper, an ancient black religious book containing a marker of purple ribbon embroidered in silver
thread with a cross. Except for this worn devotional
book, everything about her was new. A novel and sur-
prising air of opulence surrounded the shrivelled form
that for so many years had gone its ineffectual ways
muffled in shabby, shapeless coverings of wool. The
comfortable chaise-longue upon which she reclined was
new, as were also the thick, light, fleecy rug over her knees
and the black dress of excellent stuff. It was also possible
to detect some slight change in her face, a faint lightening
of its habitual expression of nervous apprehension, as
though a film of anxiety had been removed.

She closed the book and put it carefully into a sort of
pocket under the arm of the chair. This action drew her
attention to the chair itself which was still enough of a
novelty to occupy her mind for several seconds with an
appreciation of its comfort and convenience. How simple
it was not to lose one's book or one's ball of wool when
these articles could be slipped into such a handy receptacle.
Her undirected gaze dwelt with vague pleasure upon the

lawn in front of her, bright green after a wet summer, freshly cut, and adorned by the sunshine with myriads of microscopic jewels of light. It was the lawn that Frederick Henzell had prized so highly on account of its weedlessness. As she thought of her dead husband, facile tears came into her eyes.

'Now, now — no sad thoughts, Mrs. Henzell, on this beautiful day!'

A kind-faced, middle-aged woman in nurse's uniform had come from the house with a cup of Bovril on a tray. Having watched her swallow the drink, made sure that the sun was not in her eyes, and uttered a few commonplace sentences, the nurse vanished once more. Her attentions were pleasing to Marion Henzell. It was gratifying to the old woman to feel herself so important, so well cared for, the centre of such competent solicitude. The nurse's personality, too, was sympathetic to her: she was not too young and not too old, efficient but not too professional in her manner, cheerful but not unduly so. Mrs. Henzell at last felt as she had all her life wished to feel: protected, relieved of all responsibility, independent without being alone.

Presently she observed another figure coming in her direction. This time it was her daughter who was approaching. Celia had been staying at Desborough House to attend her father's funeral and to see that everything was satisfactorily arranged for her mother's future. Frederick Henzell had turned out to be a much wealthier man than anyone had supposed. The money which he had accumulated during a lifetime of unremitting, conscientious labour and concealed behind a screen of parsimoniousness and rigid economy, could no longer be hidden from the world after his death. The solicitor had left about forty thousand pounds. Out of this estate a legacy of three hundred a year was bequeathed to Celia; the remainder to go to Marion Henzell until her death when it would pass on to the daughter.

It was exceedingly hard for Mrs. Henzell to realize that she was now comparatively rich, that it was no longer necessary to pinch and scrape over the housekeeping, that the fire which heated the bath water could be alight every day instead of only three days a week as in her husband's time. Celia had tried to persuade her to leave Desborough House and to move into a smaller, gayer and more convenient home; but this she would not do. The gloomy old house where she had spent so many dreary, dissatisfied years now, at the last, had woven itself inextricably into the thin grey fabric of her waning existence. Here walked the two ghosts of those who had dominated her narrow life, here grew the ivy from her son's grave, here she would remain until she too joined them in the quiet company of death.

When Celia saw that her mother was determined to stay where she was, she had gvien in to her wishes and engaged a nurse and servants to look after her and old Mattie who was now past all except the lightest of duties. Although she had advocated a move, Celia was privately rather relieved that it would not be necessary to embark upon the project of finding a new home. She had already spent much longer than she liked in Jessington and she was eager to resume her own personal life which had been interrupted by the solicitor's death. It was not as if her mother desired or needed her company, she thought, as she came into the garden to say good-bye. They had never been accustomed to each other's society. The old woman would be perfectly contented living out her invalid's routine with her nurse, her memories, and her small physical comforts.

Seeing Celia coming towards her, Mrs. Henzell felt astonished, as she always did, to think that this well-dressed, effective, confident-looking stranger should actually be her own daughter. Two or three times lately she had tried to reckon up Celia's age, but she was shaky on dates these days, and it always seemed to her at the end of the calculation that she must have made a mistake in the year of her birth. 'She can't be thirty-eight — thirty-nine next birthday . . . it can't be so long ago . . . She doesn't look much more than twenty-five.'

Celia walked briskly across the lawn in her well-fitting green suit towards her mother's chair. She wore no hat, and her slightly curling, bright hair was like a soft flame in the sun. She announced cheerfully that she had come to say good-bye. Her car was at the front door on the other side of the house: she was going to drive herself back to Stone.

Marion Henzell was not sorry that Celia was going away. She was, in fact, rather looking forward to being left alone to the enjoyment of her new luxury. The presence of her daughter was always rather disturbing. Nevertheless, at the prospect of parting her eyes grew moist, her hands began to pluck at her skirt and to make queer little clutching movements like the claws of a bird.

'To think that he should have been the one to go first . . . and he always so strong . . . never a day's illness . . . while I . . . Why wasn't I taken?'

Celia spoke comfortingly to her. She spoke in an indulgent, indifferent tone, not thinking of what she was saying. Her thoughts had already detached themselves from Desborough House, like seagulls sailing over the crest of a hill, pursuing their own secret course, free and inviolable. All the time she was talking she was conscious of the mystery of her own individuality. No one could approach her inmost self. Her essential solitude was absolute. This gave her a peculiar feeling of power.

Soon Celia was sitting alone in the car, driving away
from Jessington. The sunlit country unfurled itself like
two gay rolls of patterned fabric on either side, the sky
was overflowing with brightness, the engine hummed
busily. Celia began to sing to herself. She felt happy and
strong. She felt, too, a new sense of financial security and
independence — a sense that her life was flowing on
strongly and propitiously towards a desirable goal. She
need no longer depend upon Francis Temple in any way.
With her pension added to the money she earned by her
writing and her father's legacy, she would be quite
comfortably off.

The death of her father had left her richer by more
than three hundred a year. She felt liberated, as if some
old curse had been lifted. Desborough House no longer
had any power to depress her. Catching sight of her
reflection in the driving mirror she smiled slightly, putting
back a strand of brilliant hair behind her left ear. It was
good that Sutherland admired her hair so much. John
Sutherland the publisher, important, rich and well-known,
tall, forceful and vigorous, with a sort of ecclesiastical
impressiveness, was a vital image in her mind. Beside this
image, the familiar likeness of Francis Temple appeared
faded, elderly and asthenic. She thought of Francis
tolerantly, but with some contempt. He was no longer
necessary to her. The wheels bearing her towards him
hummed a monotonous chant. 'What a dull life I've been
leading,' she said aloud, suddenly, as if the realization had
only just dawned on her.

Although Celia thought of Francis Temple in this somewhat derogatory way, he was, as a matter of fact, exceedingly well-preserved for a man of his age. His spare, agile figure was of the type which wears well, his fastidious, debonair look did not alter, and the only treacherous sign of advancing years was to be seen in his hair which was now altogether grey and quite thin on the top.

He was waiting at Little Stone rather impatiently for her return, for, during her absence, he had received an important piece of information: his wife had just died and he was at last free to re-marry. As soon as Celia came into the house he started to tell her this news, standing up and putting his hands in the pockets of his jacket in such a way as to draw it tightly round him, thus emphasizing his still slender waist. She listened to him without any comment, also standing, and arranging her hair in front of the looking-glass which had replaced the Bonham portraits over the mantelpiece. When he had come to the end of what he was saying there was rather an awkward pause. Celia remained silent. They were alone in the house except for the servant, hidden and unheard in the kitchen. Isabel and Clare had gone out. A sense of anti-climax slowly distilled itself into the quiet room.

Francis took his hands out of his pockets, picked up from the desk the long white envelope that had come from the lawyers with the news of his wife's death, looked at it, and then put it down again. His manner displayed an unaccustomed hesitancy.

'So, you see, there's nothing to prevent our marriage any longer,' he said finally.

Celia turned away from the mirror and looked at him.

'No.'

'I could get a special licence any day now.'

She smiled slightly.

'Yes. It's a pity . . . I've always suspected that it would happen like this . . . When it was too late.'

She went over to the window and looked out. The big house on the hill had a flimsy appearance. Everything seemed to her to wear a look of unnatural flatness and un-reality, as though a theatrical drop-scene had taken the place of the landscape.

If Francis were disappointed, mortified, surprised or in any way discomposed, he concealed the fact well. He laughed and then lighted a cigarette.

'Perhaps it is a bit late in the day to think about marriage. Anyhow, I'm at your disposal, as ever.'

He drew the smoke through his ivory holder, his usual jaunty air only just perceptibly diminished. Celia stood by the window. The face of the publisher Sutherland, with the powerful profile that always made her think of Cardinal Wolsey, floated once more in front of her mind's eye.

DR. HUGH BARRINGTON had spent several dull, expedient, economical though not professionally lucrative months in Stone, acting as locum for Dr. Turner who had gone away on a long cruising holiday. The time had slipped by with the speed engendered by a monotonous and not disagreeable routine, but now, at the end of the summer, he was glad to think that he would soon be leaving the village for ever. At the beginning of October he would be going to his own new practice in Jessington which he fully intended to build up into the most important practice in that respectable town.

Hugh Barrington was a persevering, determined and uncomplicated young man. He possessed the type of brain, sound but not at all brilliant, that harbours only one object at a time. This object he would pursue undeviatingly, and the chances were that he would gain it through sheer persistence. He had an excellent opinion of himself without being exactly conceited. He was very much the centre of his own universe. The object that was constantly present in his mind was success in his chosen profession. It was a safe bet that he would achieve it: why not? He was starting well; he had not rushed in a hurry into the first opening that had come along, but had prudently saved up his money until he could afford to buy himself a really promising practice. His qualifications were good. He was industrious, ambitious, young; the possessor of an agreeable presence and boundless physical energy.

As he walked up the rectory drive in the strong sunlight he looked as he felt — satisfied with himself and the circumstances of his existence. He was a big man — he had played rugger for his hospital — and his large face with its reddish summer tan was handsome in rather a fleshy way. He was walking because he was fond of exercise and because it had not seemed worth while getting into his car to drive the short distance between Dr. Turner's house where he was living and the rectory where he had just been attending the vicar's sister who was recovering from a heart attack. To-day everything appeared to him in an exceptionally pleasant light because it was the first of September, and his new life in Jessington suddenly seemed to have come a step nearer with the new month. He walked with an effortless stride, holding in one hand a small case so light that he was unaware of its weight, and surveying the landscape and his own future with the same feeling of satisfaction.

Although he had not been particularly discontented in Stone he was delighted to think that he would soon be going away. It had been a dull summer; infernally dull. And the country people seemed to be as dull as their ailments. He had only met one really attractive, really interesting woman the whole time he had been in the place, and he had not been able to see as much of her as he would have liked.

When he began to think about Celia Bonham his expression lost the merest fraction of its good-natured complacency. There had been a time, when he first came to Stone and before he had quite got the hang of village affairs, when he had been in danger of seeing a great deal too much of Celia. She had called him in for some trifling indisposition, and he had succumbed immediately to her bright-haired charm which shone with such spectacular effect in the wilderness of country dullness. She had invited him to dinner, and a certain growth of intimacy had rapidly flourished between them. The young man, rather bored, rather lonely, had been fascinated; he had almost lost his head. He shuddered now to think how near he had come to committing an indiscretion that might have damaged his precious career. It would have been fatal for him to get himself mixed up in a scandal with the most talked-of woman in the district. There had been some unpleasant gossip as it was. Fortunately, he had been warned in time. He had come to his senses and curtailed his visits to Little Stone — not without regrets.

No doubt about it, Celia was a dangerous woman, the sort of woman it didn't do for a young man who valued his future to see very much of. It was not as though there had ever been the least chance that she would become his wife. Once, in the days when she had first swept him off his feet, he had ventured to hint at marriage, only to be answered by an indulgent laugh. Now he could thank his lucky stars that she had not taken him seriously. A wife of the right sort would be an asset to him. In fact, it seemed almost essential that he should soon marry some nice girl whose photograph, in a large silver frame, could stand on the desk in his consulting room. But looking coolly at things he could see well enough that a woman who had been twice widowed — a woman ten years his senior, who was becoming quite well known as a writer, and who possessed, moreover, a singularly striking appearance and an unconventional reputation, was not at all a suitable wife for a young general practitioner just embarking on his career.

Nevertheless, Celia still, from time to time, occupied a prominent place in his thoughts. It was natural that her image should come more vividly before him as he passed through the green gate at the end of the rectory drive and saw the thick hedge of Little Stone a short distance ahead.

His general sense of well-being, combined with the knowledge that his sojourn at Stone was so nearly over, made him decide to relax the caution which had lately kept him away from the ivy covered house behind that high box hedge. He suddenly started to walk towards it instead of going straight across the green to the doctor's house. He had not seen Celia for over a fortnight. He would look in for a few minutes now. Surely no one could see anything scandalous in his paying her a short visit in the middle of the afternoon; besides, there seemed to be no one about. The green was completely deserted, awash with sunlight. The churchyard exhaled a dusty, drowsy, religious scent as he passed by.

Hugh Barrington walked up the brick path between the holly tree and the clipped yew. The front door was wide open and after a moment's hesitation he went inside. His careful nature disapproved slightly of the house being left so unprotected. 'Anybody might walk in,' he thought. The hall was like a dim cave after the blazing sun. Someone was standing near the foot of the stairs. His dazzled eyes faintly distinguished the gleam of fair hair and a light summer dress as he put his attaché case down on the floor. Then he went across, took the cool feminine hand and kissed it. This was a gesture Celia herself had taught him.

'I've been longing to see you again,' he said, bringing the words out impulsively.

There was a peculiar little moment. The young doctor's eyes, becoming accustomed to the semi-darkness, perceived that although the eyes looking back at him might have been Celia's eyes, neither the face nor the hair belonged altogether to Celia. A second passed, and it was borne in upon him that the hand which he held was the hand of Clare Bryant.

In a situation that would have proved highly disconcerting to most people, Hugh Barrington was supported by his invincible assurance. Certainly, he did not feel, as he generally did, that everything concerning him was going on exactly as it should do, but he did not allow himself to lose his presence of mind. Instead of being overcome by embarrassment, he sensibly began to think how best he could extricate himself from an awkward predicament without appearing foolish. Instantaneously he reached the conclusion that he must not let it appear that he had made a mistake. He did not, therefore, release Clare's passive hand, but continued to hold it and to look into her face which, now that he could discern it fairly clearly, seemed to express no surprise, no pleasure, no distaste. This lack of expression puzzled him considerably. It seemed unnatural and baffling. He could not imagine what the girl was thinking.

Of course, he had seen Clare a good many times, but he had never paid any special attention to her. Celia had monopolized his interest to such an extent that he barely noticed the daughter who, if he thought about her at all, seemed to him only a pale and immature replica of her mother.

All these reflections passed through his mind in a flash as he stood holding Clare's unresponsive hand. Suddenly the drawing-room door opened and Celia herself stepped into the hall. Her smooth face showed no more trace of feeling than that of her daughter, though the sight of the two linked hands must have surprised her.

'Hugh! How nice of you to come and see us again,' she said in her cool voice, smiling, and coming towards them.

The young man turned away from Clare to the mother with disguised relief.

Clare suddenly began touching her hair — a fair lock had fallen forward across her cheek and the right side of her forehead. Her eyes were green in the reflected light that came through the open door. She looked at Celia rather oddly. It was one of those occasions when everything about her mother — her appearance, her poise, her serenity — for some reason aroused a feeling of antagonism in the girl's heart. Celia returned her gaze with faint mockery for an instant before giving her hand to the visitor.

'Ask Rose to bring the tea, will you, Clare?'

'All right. I'll see about it at once,' Clare said, and walked quickly away to the kitchen.

CELIA was full of a sense of well-being, almost of triumph. Both mentally and physically she felt at the height of her powers. The book which she had almost finished seemed the best work she had ever done, all the time she was working she wrote effortlessly and with sureness, force and satisfaction. When she looked in the mirror her reflection pleased her profoundly. She derived an indescribable narcissistic delight from the sight of her pale, unlined, enigmatic face with its wreath of soft, brilliant curls. She was looking better than she had ever done before. It seemed to her that in some mysterious way she was immune from the years, age could not touch her; she was ageless. The general progress of her life, too, gratified her extremely. From grief and misfortune she had advanced steadily to security and fulfilment. Now she felt that the propitious climax was at hand. She was strong, full of an inexhaustible energy, prepared to move mountains.

She was staying at Stone only to finish her book. In a week or two the last words would be written and she would go to London, to John Sutherland who would marry her and translate her to the world of affluence, fame and popularity which was her proper sphere. She had finished with Little Stone. It had served its turn and she would discard it and its owner from her life without a qualm, almost without a thought, just as she had discarded Francis Temple when she had no further use for him.

Everything was clear and definite in her mind with one single exception. The exception was her young daughter, Clare. What was to be done with her? Clare would soon be eighteen. When she had left school at the end of the spring term, the head mistress had suggested that she should go on to the university. It appeared that she was considered more than usually intelligent, although she did not seem talented in any one particular way. Celia did not approve of this idea which would, she considered, involve her in a great deal of unnecessary expense. At the back of her mind, hardly recognized, was a twenty-one-year-old memory; the memory of the night at Desborough House when Frederick Henzell had rejected her own urgent appeal to be allowed to go up to Oxford. Why should she grant to her daughter an opportunity which she herself had been ruthlessly denied? This was her repressed thought. Consciously, she told herself that the girl did not really want to go on studying. Clare was not at all enthusiastic about the idea: in fact, she seemed to be singularly devoid of any sort of enthusiasm for anything. It would be a sheer waste of money to pay her fees at college.

What then was to happen to her? A grown-up daughter obviously had no part in Celia's design for successful living. She could not go to John Sutherland encumbered with a great girl of eighteen — a silent, moody girl, moreover; a girl of no special attractions.

Of course, she could leave Clare at Stone with Isabel Bonham. But this idea, too, she regarded with disfavour. It would seem altogether too much like a victory for Isabel; for was it not exactly what Isabel had always hoped for?

If only the girl had been more enterprising, more independent, it would have been possible to launch her on some sort of career. But Clare appeared to be hopelessly wanting in initiative. She did not seem to wish to do anything except to sit and read or to roam aimlessly about the hills by herself.

Celia felt nothing but irritation when she thought of this girl whom she had never been able to regard as anything but a burden, incomprehensibly thrust upon her by fate. 'She's never liked me,' she said to herself, looking out of the window at Clare who had just strolled into the garden with a book in her hand. The thought did not seem to indict her, but to free her from all responsibility. Clare moved gracefully, but to Celia she appeared to walk with an affected languor.

She abandoned her work and continued to watch Clare through the window. An idea which, like a mole, had been burrowing since yesterday in the depths of her mind, slowly worked its way to the surface. A picture nebulously shaped itself before her; a picture of Clare and the young doctor standing with joined hands in the shadowy hall. The picture faded and was replaced by others as her embryonic project developed and gained strength.

'That's it!' she murmured finally, under her breath. 'That's what I'll do.'

She went out into the garden which lay as if spent by the long summer, silent and still under the dazzling sky. No breeze rustled; the leaves drooped towards the earth. As she went, she repeated like a magic formula the words: 'That's what I'll do.' She felt almost exalted. The sense of her own power was so great that she did not doubt for a second her ability to bring about the consummation which she desired.

Meanwhile she approached her daughter who was sitting on the grass, leaning against the trunk of a cherry tree. The sun shining through the foliage enmeshed her in a net of greenish shadows and tremulous threads of light.

'What are you reading?'

Clare did not answer, but silently held out the book. Her mother glanced at the title.

'You're always reading these Russians. You read too many gloomy books altogether. You'll be getting morbid ideas about life.' Celia spoke in a light, friendly tone. 'It's a pity it's so dull for you here. Anyway, I'm glad Hugh Barrington's coming round this afternoon. I thought we'd drive up Lads Hill and take our tea into the woods.' She paused for a moment. 'He's rather deserted us lately, hasn't he? But I thought he wouldn't be able to keep away from you long.'

'What do you mean?' Clare asked, as though suddenly recalled from a dream. Celia looked at her inscrutably. Her hair burned in the sun like an enchantress's diadem of small flames.

'You know you're the person he's interested in here.'

'Oh — do you think so?'

Clare suddenly seemed to have become confused, almost startled. Her straying glance was both agitated and vague. She put up her hand and pushed back her heavy hair — a gesture which always annoyed Celia.

'Yes, of course he comes to see you. You're the only young girl he has a chance of talking to in the place,' she said almost crossly, turning away and starting to pick some sprays of Michaelmas daisy from the herbaceous border near by.

Clare got up and wandered indoors. She wanted to be alone. She went to her bedroom which was in the front of the house, closed the door, and stood looking out of the window towards Great Stone. She looked intently at the big house, and her heart felt heavy. How lonely it seemed at Stone without Isabel! Isabel had been away nearly a week now, nursing a sick relative in the north, a lonely, friendless old woman, upon whom she had taken pity. Clare had received a letter from her that morning, saying that she would be back soon but that she could not leave Cousin Charlotte for a few days longer.

The girl sighed. During the years she had been at school she had made friends, she had felt busy and content. But now that she was back at Stone her school life seemed unreal, like an interlude, or like a holiday that had no proper place in the pattern of her existence. Now she had come back to her real life, she felt lonely and empty, and that was her natural state. Little Stone felt empty, too. Isabel was away, and Francis Temple had vanished as unobtrusively as he had arrived. Soon Celia would depart, and then it seemed to her that she would be left quite alone.

Her eyes dilated and changed, reflecting a memory. Outside everything floated in sunshine, the countless, shimmering leaves were still green, and yet a sense of approaching autumn pervaded the day like a fugitive perfume, indefinable, thrilling and sad. Why was it that all lovely things were blended with sadness? Of course, Celia talked so queerly, one shouldn't take her seriously, she often didn't mean what she said. Probably it was all nonsense. But he had held her hand, he had looked into her face in the dark hall, and a strange, ecstatic entrancement had come over her, as though she would like to stand there for ever, just feeling her hand in his. The extraordinary comfort that had filled her heart because of that contact with another human being! She knew that she must feel it again, that, like a drug-taker, she would never be satisfied until she had repeated that unique and trance-like sensation.

Clare looked up at the sky where two separate armies of cloud were staging their innocuous manœuvres on the azure field. High up in the zenith trailed the transparent wind clouds, tenuous pearly scarves, wreaths, veils, laces and nets, while lower down sailed, flock-like, small, dazzling bodies of white in interminable array. She closed her eyes for a moment, and a feeling came to her as though the cells of her body were dissolving, as though she were becoming lighter than air and might soon float away, up into those airy cloud lands.

HUGH BARRINGTON had once more become a frequent
visitor at Little Stone. He was not any less cautious, nor
had he lost sight of the main object of his career; but he
no longer felt himself endangered by Celia, her proximity
was no longer a perilous stimulus to his senses or a threat
to his peace of mind. Celia herself had helped him to
achieve this new attitude. Although she was still charming to him whenever they met, there was now a slight,
indefinable change in her conduct towards him. She made
it clear in some way that she was not accessible. She had
somehow established their relationship on a much safer
basis; a basis of pleasant, unemotional companionship.

The young man saw a great deal more of Clare than
he had done in the past. After the initial episode that had
brought her in front of his notice, it was impossible for
him to be unaware of her. He was inclined on the whole
to regard her with favour. Although she was quite overshadowed by her mother in every fascinating quality, she
yet seemed to possess a certain quiet charm of her own.
On the occasions when he had happened to be left alone
with her, he had not found her company disagreeable.
She herself had little to say, but she was a good listener,
and her look of serious attention was pleasing to his
conceit.

This afternoon as Hugh walked up the brick path he
found the front door shut. The earlier part of the day
had been wet. Now it had stopped raining, but the air
was much colder and the sky was covered with a dull, even
blanket of grey. There was a chilly smell of wet leaves

and of incipient decay. A little rain water had collected in the hollow of the worn stone in front of the door, where it lay like a tarnished mirror reflecting the leaden sky.

A fire had been lighted in the drawing-room and Celia was standing beside it. Isabel had not yet returned from the north and Clare was not in the room.

'A fire — that looks cheerful!' The young man smiled gaily and complacently as though the one thing needed to complete his satisfaction with the way the world was going had been the sight of a fire. With his long stride he walked to the fireplace and stood watching the flames with rather prominent eyes. 'Yes, it really feels like autumn to-day.'

'Are you glad the summer's over?' Celia asked.

Straightening his dark purple tie, he crossed the room with the same swinging stride and moved the tea-table into position for Rose who had just carried in the tray.

'I'm looking forward to starting work on my own,' he answered, as the maid left the room.

Celia was smoking a cigarette in an amber holder.

'We shall miss you,' she said, letting a curl of smoke escape slowly between her lips. ' . . . Clare especially. I don't know what she'll do with herself when you've gone. I believe she's half in love with you.'

Hugh was struck by these words, lightly and, as it were, jokingly uttered. But before he had thought of a reply, Clare herself entered the drawing-room.

'So there you are!' Celia said with a smile. 'I was just telling Hugh how lonely we shall be after he's gone away.'

The girl was displeased by her mother's remark. A hot, painful wave passed over her, though her face and hands remained cold.

The silver kettle on the tea-tray was singing over its

tiny flame. In the sides of the silver kettle, in the tea-pot, in the milk jug and in the sugar basin, the red heart of the fire glowed like a cheerful jewel reflected in many diminished contortions, but the cold grey light of the day still dominated the room. Clare felt awkward and gloomy. She greeted the visitor briefly and sat down near the table. She suddenly felt overwhelmed with hatred at the sight of Celia's smooth hand, adorned with a large opal ring, gracefully and efficiently lifting the kettle and pouring water into the tea-pot.

She did not hear what the others were saying. Their words buzzed in the room and made no more impression upon her than the buzzing of flies. Her thoughts surrounded her like a dark cloud.

Hugh Barrington, in response to a question from Celia, was describing the house in which he was going to start his professional life in Jessington. He described the rooms minutely, with enjoyment and much detail. The topic was of absorbing interest to him, and it did not cross his mind that anyone else might find the recital tedious. When he came to the description of his consulting room, which included an adjustable couch of the very latest design and a cabinet fitted with hot and cold water, he suddenly remembered the silver framed photograph which seemed to him an almost essential part of the room's equipment. Glancing across the table, it occurred to him that a photograph of Clare, taken as she looked to-day, with her hair softer and fluffier than usual, would suit the silver frame quite well. Photographed in a white dress, her wedding dress, perhaps, and carrying some flowers, she would, if touched up a little, make a grave, innocent, almost angelic picture. Celia's joking words, 'I believe she's half in love with you', kept running like a refrain at the back of his mind. He began to feel restless — a most unusual feeling for him — and though he did not lose the thread of what he was saying, the conversation no longer seemed so absorbing.

About half-past five he got up to go, explaining to Celia that he had to be in the surgery by six o'clock. Clare had slipped out of the room a few minutes earlier and was nowhere to be seen. Her absence caused him a slight pang of disappointment or of relief — he, unanalytical, could not have said which it was. Then, just as he was opening the hand gate in the hedge, he saw her coming round the path at the side of the house. She was wearing a coat, and a bright yellow scarf was knotted loosely round her neck.

'Hullo! Where are you going?' he asked.

'I'm going for a walk.'

Hugh Barrington unlatched the gate and held it open. 'Walk across the green with me,' he said to her.

Clare agreed impassively, but a curious cloudy look came into her eyes. They walked off side by side, in the autumnal late afternoon.

The sky was more threatening now. Immense black shapes, like the bodies of whales, moved slowly across it, herded on by the clammy wind. The declining light was misty and grey. Clare walked as if in a dream. It seemed to her that she was conscious of the man beside her not with her brain only, but with every bone, muscle and nerve of her entire body. Her hair blew in the wind.

'Your hair looks different to-day,' he said, smiling down at her. He was considerably taller than she.

'I washed it last night.'

Together they traversed the open space about which the cottages clustered like a ring of brown, sleeping beasts. The dismal light turned the grass a sour acid green, ruffled like fur by the wind. Clare was almost silent. Hugh talked somewhat inconsecutively. A feeling of repressed excitement had communicated itself to him from her. He kept glancing down at the yellow scarf which seemed to burn with an unnatural, almost flamy brilliance in the grey light, at the thick, blowing hair over which he wanted to pass his hand. Once she turned her head slightly to meet his eyes, her strange eyes gazed straight into his for an instant, cloudy with obscure emotion. He felt his excitement mounting.

'Tell me, Clare; was it true what your mother said — that you'll miss me after I've gone?'

Clare did not answer immediately. A farm labourer passed them on his way home from work, an old man, bent and dressed in dun coloured clothes matching the day. He touched his cap and plodded on with a dull gait.

'Yes, of course we shall miss you. We have so few friends here.'

Something in the case which the young man carried kept making a small chinking sound. They reached Dr. Turner's house — a plain, smallish building at the end of a short drive. A hedge of enormous laurels grew on each side of the entrance. Hugh Barrington opened the gate. They both passed through and then stopped. Here it was already dusk. They were in the shadow of the ancient laurels; the light lay coldly on the tops of the leaves, but the under sides were blackly shaded. The wooden gate divided from the green the spot where their two figures were standing. The drive ended at the dark little house. The huge laurels, towering above them, concealed the village, the landscape and the wing-like curve of the hill.

'It seems gloomy here this evening,' Clare said. 'You

must be glad to be going away.' She paused. 'I've always been happy living at Stone, but somehow, just now, for the first time, I wish I were going away too.' She looked up at him. 'I feel sad to-day . . . I suppose it's because winter's coming — '

Hugh Barrington's brain was busily at work. He was trying to recall some talk he had heard recently in Jessington about Clare's grandfather who had died, leaving his widow a comfortable fortune. The old woman was an invalid, he seemed to remember. Probably she wouldn't last long. The money, presumably, would go to Celia next. But Celia appeared to be quite well-off already — doubtless she would make suitable provision for her only child when she inherited the solicitor's estate. In the semi-darkness under the laurels he could not see Clare's wide eyes, but the nervous excitement which radiated from her still affected him.

'Dear little Clare.'

He approached her and put his attaché case on the ground. A faint antiseptic smell, an exudation of health and confidence, came to her from his large young body.

'How would you like to come to — come to Jessington with me?'

Clare trembled. Her eyes suddenly grew moist and shining. Hugh took her hand.

'What do you mean?' she asked faintly.

'I want to take you away with me for good. I want to marry you. Don't you understand?'

He stood very close to her — tall, athletic, with confident smiling mouth. His large, clean hands firmly clasped her cold fingers; he stood beside her the personification of optimism and normality, of hearty masculine well-being. Clare felt entranced, as if drugged. He put

228

his arms round her and kissed her with warm satisfaction. Confused thoughts of Celia, of money, of a photograph in a silver frame, blended with more sensual images in his mind.

Clare no longer thought of anything. Her heart beat quickly, she trembled, and clung to the coat from which emanated a faint smell of tobacco and disinfectant. She was in that state of dreamlike beatitude when consciousness seems almost lost. She had forgotten Isabel whom she had loved for so long, and only knew that for the first time she was identified with another living creature, the same, and yet not the same, as herself. Hugh's body felt to her at that moment like an extension of her own being. She felt that she had merged herself in his strength. A glorious sense of fulfilment flooded her lonely heart.

AT eleven o'clock at night Hugh Barrington entered the
room which he had used as his bedroom during the
period he had spent in Dr. Turner's house. It was the
last night he would sleep in that room, his last night in
Stone, his last night as a single man. To-morrow he was
to marry Clare Bryant in the little church on the other
side of the green. Directly after the wedding they would
go to Jessington, to move into the house where, in a few
days, he was to begin his independent professional career.
He had been prepared, if necessary, to devote those few
days to Clare. But she, knowing the way his interests
centred in Jessington, had rejected the idea of a brief
honeymoon and expressed herself willing to settle straight
away into her new home. The young man was gratified
by this decision. He considered that it showed good
sense and a praiseworthy attention to his wishes, auguring
well for the future.

His luggage was packed, the room had a gloomy,
impersonal look, ponderously garnished with Dr. Turner's
Victorian furniture. Hugh was not very sensitive to his
surroundings, but he had never cared for the room.
There was something about hanging his clothes in another
man's wardrobe that offended his strong sense of personal
ownership. He rejoiced to think that to-morrow night
he would sleep in his own bed, and that he would not
sleep alone.

He went to the window and looked out in the direction
of Little Stone. The night was pitch dark, cloudy, and

full of wind. He could see nothing at all except the agitated black mass of laurels looming up close at hand.

Yes, it was uncommonly sensible of Clare to be ready to go straight to Jessington, he reflected. There would certainly be a lot to do in the house, and it was an excellent plan to get everything settled and in good running order before he actually started work.

It looked as though Clare were going to turn out docile and reasonable. On the whole he was very satisfied with his bargain. There had been one or two bad moments when he had reproached himself for acting impulsively. Once or twice, too, an uneasy, indefinable suspicion of Celia had crossed his mind. He had occasionally received a vague impression that her attitude was not so simple, open and amicable as it appeared to be on the surface. When he examined these suspicions they seemed to evaporate. Now he thought that he had banished them for good and all.

A contented smile came on his face as he contemplated his future bride. The girl seemed to have grown prettier during the last few days, she had an air about her, she would do him credit in Jessington society. Of course, she would never have her mother's striking appearance, but that, in any case, was hardly desirable in a doctor's wife who must, pre-eminently, appear respectable. It was a pity that there should have been this scandal about Celia. But, after all, Jessington was a good way from Stone. The bad effect of any rumours of Celia's eccentricities which might have travelled so far would be cancelled out by the fact that Clare was the granddaughter of a man well known and respected in the town. On her own account, the girl should make a good impression. Her youthfulness was appealing. Moreover, at her age she was unlikely to have any set ideas. He would be able to mould her to his own pattern. Most young girls were amenable, and she appeared specially so.

A yellow light suddenly flowered far off in the rushing darkness. It came from an upper window of Little Stone. Hugh Barrington watched it for a moment; then, growing cold, turned away and started to undress. Soon he was lying stretched out on the old-fashioned mahogany bed. Lying on his back, he yawned once. All his thoughts started to slide together into the warm, comfortable abyss that received him so quickly and so unfailingly every night. Just at the last, before sleep submerged him entirely, there floated before his mind a face which, oddly enough, was not Clare's face at all, but another more vivid countenance, crowned by a coronet of brilliant hair.

In the house on the other side of the green, Clare did not fall asleep so quickly as the young doctor. She was in a nervous state somewhere between exaltation and distress. To start with, her dominant feeling was one of almost ecstatic excitement, of wonder, of joy. It was hard to believe that she, who had recently felt herself destined to sadness and solitude, was actually experiencing such happy emotions.

Yes, she was wonderfully happy, but at the same time she was obscurely perturbed. Her perturbation concerned Isabel. Of course, Isabel had been like a mother to her and she loved her as much as ever, but for the first time a barrier seemed to have come between them. She could not have explained why it was that from the very moment when Hugh had first taken her hand in the hall the barrier had been there. Again and again an impulse had come to her to write describing her emotions to Isabel from whom she had never kept any secret. Yet somehow the letter had not been written. It was as if she anticipated Isabel's disapproval. Or was it that she felt guilty about deserting her friend?

Uneasy thoughts accumulated in Clare's mind. There was no evading the fact that she had behaved badly towards Isabel, withholding her confidence, and leaving the elder woman to bear the unsoftened shock of the news when she returned to Little Stone. Isabel had been kind and gentle as ever; she had said very little, but her eyes had been full of anxiety. 'Are you quite sure that you love each other?' she had asked. 'Do be quite certain . . . All I want in life now is your happiness.' Clare could not forget the intensity with which those sad eyes had dwelt upon her, full of endless, selfless devotion, full of sympathy and also of apprehension.

She got out of bed and went to the window. In the black, windy night a wan beam rested upon the grass — the light from Isabel's room. 'She's still awake, then,' Clare thought. 'She's thinking about me — worrying . . . I ought to go to her.' But instead of doing any such thing she went back to her bed and lay down again.

Even now she did not fall asleep very quickly. She kept thinking of to-morrow, of Isabel, of the strange new sensations which Hugh Barrington had awakened in her. Presently the image of the young man drove all others out of her mind. 'He makes me feel safe . . . happy,' she thought drowsily. Other words rose disconnectedly, like bubbles coming to the surface of a deep pool. 'Jessington . . . the house . . . wife . . . I'll do anything for him,' she thought with a kind of touching gratitude for his love. In the darkness her pale face grew soft, vulnerable and submissive. Isabel was forgotten.

THE spring sun had once more brought out the blossom on the flowering trees in the Jessington gardens. White petals drifted lightly like snowflakes in the warm wind, daffodils and hyacinths crowded everywhere, in flower-beds and window-boxes, and on barrows and stalls in the streets. Only the garden of Desborough House was flowerless, and even here the damp grass was a beautiful vivid green that glowed like a jewel. Birds were singing and hopping about in the bushes as Clare walked towards the high wooden gate that ended the drive of her grandmother's house. It was the first Friday in April, and she had just had tea with the old lady, as she had done nearly every Friday since she had been living in Jessington.

Clare was not fond of her grandmother. Marion Henzell, wizened and frail, secluded in her tiny invalid's world, with her fluttering, indistinct gestures and speech, seemed scarcely like a human being to the young girl. Left to herself, Clare would have avoided her. It was Hugh who had wished her to go, Hugh who had suggested the weekly tea-time visits upon which he sometimes accompanied her when he was not too busy. The practical young man thought it diplomatic to keep on good terms with his wife's wealthy relative.

Clare sighed as she passed out into the road through the door cut in the large gateway. During the six months that she had been married to the young doctor she had tried hard to please him, to turn herself into the sort of person he desired her to be. It was not an easy task, and she had not been very successful.

Hugh Barrington expected his wife to run his house expertly and economically, to take down telephone messages accurately and to book appointments, to pay calls and to entertain the right sort of people, to give dinners and tea-parties, and in general to behave in such a way as to hasten his social and professional advancement. Upheld by the consciousness of his love, it had at first seemed to Clare that she would be able to do all these things. It had appeared to her that there was nothing which she could not achieve with that strong support.

But as time went on she began to lose heart a little. She perceived that she was not doing as well as her husband expected — that she was failing him in some way. Moreover, Hugh himself seemed to be withdrawing from her. She had the impression that every day he was a little further off, a little less accessible. In his industry and his enthusiasm for his profession, in his devotion to his rapidly increasing practice, he seemed to be losing sight of Clare as his bride and to be regarding her simply as a rather inefficient helper with whom he occasionally became impatient.

She no longer felt protected and secure in his love. A sense of anxiety and strain was gradually taking possession of her. She was beginning to feel now that she would never be able to fulfil her husband's requirements. He was so busy these days that she saw very little of him, and she was starting to feel lonely and out of place, just as she had felt at Stone. 'I don't fit in here, any more than I did there,' she told herself gloomily as she walked in the sunshine.

Everything seemed worse because it was spring and the small clouds looked soft as lambswool in the blue sky. 'In April people ought to be happy.' But she was oppressed by sadness and by a feeling of failure.

To-night two guests were coming to dinner, important people upon whom it was necessary that Clare should make a good impression. As she thought of the grey solemn man and his expensively dressed wife, her heart sank. What was she to say to them, how could she win the approval of beings who seemed as remote as inhabitants of another world? 'It's hopeless ... They won't like me ... Everything's sure to go wrong, and Hugh will be angry with me again.' For the first time she really gave way to despair. It was as though a sea of depressing thoughts, which she had been holding at bay for a long time, had suddenly burst through all barriers and flooded her mind. It hardly seemed worth while making any further effort.

As a rule, when she left Desborough House, she felt a sense of relief, as though she had escaped into the fresh air from some close and unwholesome cell. But to-day, instead of walking briskly away, her footsteps lagged and she was almost inclined to turn back, as if to a sanctuary. For once she almost envied her grandmother, safe in her sickroom seclusion, unharassed by any demands from the outer world.

Starbank House, the house rented by Dr. Barrington, was near the centre of the town. To walk there from Desborough House generally took Clare about a quarter of an hour. Now she was walking much slower than usual. She walked on the sunny side of the road where the trees of neighbouring gardens overhung the pavement. The new leaves whispered gaily and secretly of spring. She reached the end of the residential road. In front lay the busier part of Jessington and the street with shops on each side of it. There were no more gardens.

Her steps quickened, and she soon reached the quiet cul-de-sac which was now her home. She could see Starbank House from some distance away. When she had first come to the house its name had pleased her, but the appearance of the building for some reason had caused her an inward chill. Now she experienced the same chilly feeling. Starbank House stood out from its neighbours because it was built of a lighter brick. It was one of those flat, face-like houses which have a watchful expression. As Clare approached, it struck her that the house seemed to sneer. She went up the steps to open the glossy front door, and the windows, veiled discreetly in muslin, eyed her with furtive contempt.

She went inside. The parlourmaid came out of the dining-room where she had been polishing the mahogany table in preparation for the evening. She wished to know which of the sets of lace or embroidered mats were to be used for the dinner party. While Clare was speaking to her she had the idea that the young woman, like the house itself, was watching her with some unspoken and contemptuous understanding. 'She sees through me,' thought the girl, without knowing exactly what the thought implied. The sensation of being out of place increased so much that she felt like an impostor and was ashamed in front of the servant. 'I've got no right to be giving orders to her,' she said to herself in confusion.

As soon as the parlourmaid had gone back to the kitchen Clare opened the door of the consulting-room. Although she knew that her husband was not in the house she instinctively sought comfort in this room filled with the aura of his confident personality. She looked at the photograph of herself which stood on the desk. A feeling of helplessness and bewilderment enveloped her as she gazed at the pictured girl in her white dress who gazed back with a somewhat lost, somewhat wistful air from the big silver frame. The photograph seemed to have the same inappropriateness of which she was aware in herself; it did not belong to the room, it was out of place. 'What does it all mean . . .?' Perhaps somewhere in the universe there was a touchstone that she had never found, perhaps there was a clue that would make everything simple and clear — if only she knew where to look. . . .

A puzzled frown came on her face, she sank deeper and deeper into a queer kind of muse in front of the photograph. At Little Stone she had felt lonely and empty, then Hugh had come and driven away her loneliness; now she was in Jessington and again she felt empty and alone.. She heard a door open and close. She did not look up. Hugh Barrington came into the room.

'What on earth are you doing in here, Clare?'

He stared at her in astonished disapproval.

'Oh . . . I'm not doing anything.'

'So I perceive. I should have thought you might have found a better occupation than standing about admiring your own photograph.'

He spoke more crossly than he intended because there was something in her attitude that was particularly repugnant to his energetic, extrovert nature. 'She looks half asleep,' flashed through his mind, unaccompanied by any sympathetic impulse. He paused for a reply, but, receiving none, continued with added vexation:

'You haven't forgotten that the Egertons are coming to dinner, I suppose?'

'No.'

'Well, have you made sure that the table has been properly laid this time? You know last week when the Seymours were here Dawes put out the wrong glasses for the hock.'

'I'll go and make sure everything's all right after I've changed my dress,' answered Clare.

'Which dress are you going to wear?'

'I thought the blue — '

Her hesitant replies irritated the young man still further. He quickly pulled out his case and lighted a cigarette, hiding his annoyance behind a cloud of smoke. It was really too bad — here was he, working his hardest to build up the practice, and what help did he get from his wife, the person above all others whom anyone would have expected to co-operate with him? Nothing but queer moods and lackadaisical looks. There was no life, no enterprise about the girl. Really, she only seemed half present most of the time. 'I've got enough to do putting up with temperamental patients without having this sort of thing in my home life,' he thought.

'No: wear the white one. It suits you better,' he said. 'And for heavens' sake try and get a little cheerfulness into your expression for once. I particularly want the Egertons to have an amusing evening — and how can you expect to entertain anybody unless you look pleasant?'

The girl hung her head. A heavy lock of hair fell forward across her cheek, and she slowly raised her hand and pushed it away. Hugh Barrington was not immune from the irritating effect of this gesture which Celia had found so exasperating in the past.

'I'm beginning to wonder why you married me,' Clare said in a low tone.

He pulled at his cigarette and breathed out an angry mouthful of smoke.

'And so am I! I sometimes think your mother must have hypnotized me. She persuaded me into it ... without my realizing what she was doing.'

'Mother persuaded you to marry me?' Clare exclaimed, in a voice that was almost a cry. She lifted her face and he saw a sudden wild light come into her strange eyes.

The young man felt that he had gone rather too far. He controlled his anger and tried to carry off the situation with a laugh.

'Oh, Good Lord, Clare! Don't be so deadly serious about everything! One can't say a word to you — you're so touchy ... Anyhow, it's time to dress now. I'm going upstairs.'

He went out of the room. Clare stood still for a few moments before slowly following him. 'He never loved me, then,' she thought to herself. 'It was mother ... I might have guessed — ' Two tears slowly filled her eyes and slid down her cheeks as she crossed the hall.

X

As Clare reached the upper landing she heard water running into the bath. Hugh was already in the bathroom. She entered the bedroom and switched on the light. The room with its two beds standing side by side looked orderly, secure and matter-of-fact, the bedroom of two people whose lives were established on a firm and respected basis. Curtains had been drawn over the windows, shutting out the disturbing, perilous beauty of the evening sky across the pale green reaches of which a fragile new moon was sailing. In the basin on the washstand stood a brass can of hot water covered by a towel.

To Clare all the familiar things which she had seen so many times before, now wore a strange aspect. The room where, long ago, as it seemed, she had spent moments of purest joy, to-night showed her a different face. She looked at the sensible, well-made furniture which her husband had chosen for its enduring qualities as well as for its pleasing appearance. The shiny wooden surfaces gave her back a blank stare. Like a sleep-walker, she went to the nearer window, pulled the curtain aside, and looked out. The slender moon-bow struck sharp as a silvery voice on her senses.

'Oh . . . the new moon! I saw it through the glass,' she thought to herself in dismay. Although she was not usually superstitious, the incident seemed ominous and she hastily let the curtain fall into place.

Turning back to the room, she opened the wardrobe and took her white evening dress from its hanger. But instead of starting to change, she laid the dress on the foot of the bed and herself sat down beside it. She shivered a little though the air was quite warm.

During the last few minutes since she had left the consulting room, a kind of dazed feeling had come over her. Now she was not even thinking of what Hugh had said. She was not thinking of anything. She was sitting on the bed when she ought to have been changing her clothes and preparing herself to entertain the important guests. She was gazing aimlessly in front of her. Splashing sounds came from the bathroom. Presently these noises ceased, the bathroom door opened, and she heard her husband's slippered steps on the landing. He went into his dressing-room. She did not stir. Through the closed communicating door she could hear him moving about. He put on his shoes, and at once his footsteps sounded confident and determined, the weighty footsteps of a man who knew where he was going and would undoubtedly arrive at his destination. Clare began to count his steps. If she closed her eyes, the steps seemed to form themselves into a pattern against a black background of emptiness. Sometimes the pattern was a simple star shape. Sometimes it wove itself into a complex mazy involution. She herself seemed to be at the centre of the maze. The idea came to her that life was the maze from which she must extricate herself, and escape . . . whither? She did not understand her own thought, but she suddenly felt drawn towards some escape, towards darkness and silence, as she sat on the bed, listening to her husband's firm steps in the next room.

All at once he opened the door and confronted her. He was fully dressed for the evening except for his black coat. His glossy white shirt front reflected the light and made his large face look red.

'Clare! Why aren't you getting dressed?' he asked, coming nearer and bringing with him his usual faint smell of antiseptics and tobacco, masked now with eau-de-Cologne. 'Why are you sitting there doing nothing?'

Clare was silent. Again he was struck by the wild, vague look in her eyes which he had noticed downstairs. 'How queer she looks', he thought with some slight uneasiness. 'What can be the matter with her?'

'Don't you feel well?'

'I don't want to come down to dinner . . . I can't — '

Her voice did not sound to him quite normal. He frowned and watched her more closely. He felt at a loss — unfamiliar sensation for him. Clare glanced straight up into his face. When he caught the empty gleam of her eyes, a flicker of repulsion passed over his healthy nerves. 'No, she certainly can't appear looking like that.'

'If you feel ill you'd better go to bed,' he said to her. 'I'll apologize and explain — it's very awkward, but I'll have to manage somehow.'

Once more he frowned, touching his neat tie and scrutinizing her closely, indignant at this tiresome and unforeseen complication of his carefully planned existence. 'I hope she's not going to have some sort of breakdown,' he thought. He did not like her appearance at all.

'You'd better go to bed,' he repeated, not knowing quite what to do.

Clare looked at him distantly and answered, after a pause: 'I shan't be able to sleep. I haven't slept much for a long time.'

'I'll give you something to make you sleep.'

He went out of the room. She sat still, profoundly indifferent, blank. She could not have told whether minutes or only seconds elapsed before he returned with a small bottle which he put down on the table beside the bed.

'Here, take one of these with a little water. You can take another one later if you don't drop off — but not more than two, mind. A good night's rest will put you right . . . I must go down now — the Egertons will be here any minute.'

He hurried away. Clare, left alone, did not move. She did not attempt to undress or to lie down, but simply remained where she was, sitting on the edge of the bed and staring at the hot water can which was slowly growing cold under its towel.

Suddenly something, she could not have said what it was, made her look at her watch. The time was five minutes past eight. They would have started dinner downstairs. A little while ago there had been sounds in the house to which she had paid no attention, the sounds of the visitors' arrival. Now all was quiet. They would be in the dining-room, sitting round the big polished table with the lace mats marking each place. But her place would be empty. Perhaps they would put the photograph from the consulting room in her place — it would do just as well. This idea made her smile.

For a few moments longer her brain continued to occupy itself with disconnected and fanciful images which vanished abruptly to give place to the first rational thought that had come to her since she reached the bedroom. 'I wonder if Dawes remembered the hock glasses?' All at once she seemed to come back to herself. She stood up and looked round the silent room with a sort of alarm. 'Why am I dreaming up here? What's wrong with me?' she muttered aloud. She pushed back the heavy hair that had fallen across her cheek. Her eyes rested upon a photograph of Hugh on the top of the chest-of-drawers. The sight of the large, handsome, fleshy face re-awoke in her heart the anguish which recently had been numbed.

'Hugh?' she said aloud, as if in incredulity, in amazement, in supplication.

The silence derided her.

'Hugh!'

Clare uttered the name once more, with urgent appeal, the neat, lighted room remained unresponsive, obdurate, mocking.

'He never loved me, then,' she thought in despair, as though a verdict had been pronounced against her.

Suddenly she was engulfed by a confused wave of horror and shame. The sight of the bed in which her husband had slept sent deep shudders over her limbs. 'I can't face him again . . . No — never . . . I must go away from him . . . Away from this house . . . at once . . . before anyone stops me — '

She hurriedly powdered her face, dragged a comb through her thick hair and fetched her hat and coat from the cupboard. Her previous inertia was now replaced by a kind of febrile activity that was quite as abnormal. The thought of packing a few things occurred to her, but she rejected it. It seemed to her that there was not an instant to be lost, that the slightest delay might prove fatal. 'Isabel will lend me whatever I need,' she reflected. The picture of Little Stone had taken shape in her mind as her sole earthly refuge.

As soon as she was ready she looked inside her handbag. The centre partition contained two one pound notes and a few coins. 'That will do — that will be enough,' she murmured. For another moment she gazed round the room as if seeking something she might have forgotten: but finally it was the bottle of tablets which Hugh had left at her bedside which she put into her bag, thinking: 'To-night, at last, I'll have a long sleep.'

XI

CLARE quietly left the bedroom and began to descend the stairs. When she reached the landing half way down the flight she paused, drawing back into the shadow and peering over the banisters. 'I must be careful not to let Dawes see me,' she thought. She heard a murmur of conversation as the dining-room door opened, and the parlourmaid came out into the hall with a tray. The young woman in her neat black and white uniform glanced in the direction of the staircase. Clare's heart leapt violently and then seemed to stand still. 'She's seen me!' she thought to herself, panic stricken. But the maid went on her way to the kitchen without another glance.

Clare hastily controlled her alarm and came to the foot of the stairs. She tiptoed across the hall. Outside the dining-room door she hesitated for a second, listening to the voices within. In spite of her anxiety to escape, some queer impulse of curiosity urged her to linger there. She could not hear the words, but she gathered from the tone that the little party was going well. Behind the closed door the voices, fabulous-sounding in their remoteness, seemed to be speaking in another dimension than hers — voices, as it were, of beings on a different plane. 'How could I possibly join in with them?' she thought: and then, sadly: 'Hugh will get on better without me.'

The noise of the front door closing behind her filled her again with acute fears. Surely someone would hear; someone would come out of the dining-room, out of the house, to restrain her. As she hurried away, she kept glancing over her shoulder with an expression of dread. But the blank face of the house remained sealed, the door like a pursed mouth that bides its time, to open the more formidably later on. The threat implicit in the shut door alarmed her more than actual pursuit would have done, and she broke into a run. One or two passers-by gave her inquisitive looks, but she did not notice them.

When she emerged from the cul-de-sac into the busier street she felt calmer. Here, on this fine evening, there were quite a number of people about. She mingled with them, slackening her pace, relieved because no one now looked at her or paid her any attention. The glare of the street lamps made the moon seem tiny and infinitely far-off. A greenish gleam, like phosphorescence, lingered on in the western sky. A garage behind a row of petrol pumps was brightly lighted. Clare went inside. A man in overalls came up to her.

'I want to hire a car,' she said to him; 'to take me to Stone.'

'Now?'

'Yes — at once.'

'It's late — we're just shutting up for the night.'

The man looked at her dubiously. His face was grimy and smeared with oil: it wore an obstructive look. Clare came nearer to him.

'I must get to Stone to-night — it's most urgent.'

She looked straight into his eyes and spoke slowly, quietly and emphatically as one would speak to a foreigner or a very stupid person who must be made to understand something important. 'I've been sent for, you see. Somebody there is ill and I'm needed at once.' It seemed to her that she was showing a great deal of cunning and resource in giving this explanation.

She was so calm, so absolutely sure of what she wanted, that the man was impressed.

'It's a long run from here,' he objected, with diminished resistance.

'Only fifteen miles. I'll pay whatever you ask.'

'All right. You wait here a minute,' he said, reluctantly giving in and going towards the back of the garage.

When she was sitting inside the car, being driven away from Jessington, she felt better, almost cheerful, as if at the eleventh hour she had escaped from a dreadful danger. She felt that she had handled the situation in the garage extremely well. Now she was barely conscious of the shabby, jolting old taxi or of the man who sat in front of her in the driver's seat, his head hidden by a greasy chauffeur's cap. They were merely the means of transporting her to Stone — the refuge for which she longed. 'Everything will be all right once I get there,' she assured herself.

The car rattled along noisily, bumping over the bad country roads. The fields were covered by the colourless cloak of night and the still leafless trees seemed to be sleeping. From the sinking moon and from the stars came an ethereal radiance. It was not so much an illumination as a spectre of light, which gave to the world a quality that was at the same time solemn, portentous and unreal, like the atmosphere of a significant dream. Clare did not seem to take much notice of this, yet the mysterious influence of the night had its effect on her, plunging her once more into an entranced state.

She was surprised when the drive came to an end. It seemed to her that only a few minutes had passed since she stood in the Jessington garage. The driver had pulled up near the inn while he opened the door to ask her to which house she wanted to go. She got out of the car, paid the man, and sent him away. Then she started to walk across the dark village green. The new moon had sunk out of sight; the enormous sky, filled with stars, stretched like a gleaming net overhead. Although it was not much after nine o'clock, the village already seemed to be deeply asleep. The cottages, the church, the farm buildings, all struck her as strangely dark and deserted. There was something sinister in the darkness. She walked on. She no longer felt as though she had escaped. Depression closed in on her. She had the sensation of having come to a place that had recently been abandoned by all its inhabitants. The dark dwellings surrounding the green had an ominous secret air. Perhaps if she entered one she would find the occupants sitting dead round the table, overtaken by some sudden, unimaginable doom. She came to the box hedge and entered the garden of Little Stone. The small house in its black ivy dress, terrifyingly silent, unlighted, seemed huddled like a mourner shrouded in grief. Tragedy seemed to invest its mum shape. A cold night breeze whispered an unpropitious message among the leaves.

Half way up the brick path Clare paused. She dared not go any farther. A terrible fear which she dared not admit to herself was beginning to clutch her heart.

'Isabel!' she called out. Her voice sounded small and thin in the boundless night. No one answered. The house remained silent and dark. Only the stirring leaves repeated like a lamentation the name, 'Isabel'.

'Isabel, I've come back — I want to come back to you!' These were the words that filled her entire consciousness, but she did not utter them aloud. 'She's gone, then ... There's no one here ... I'm quite alone,' she muttered, turning from the house in despair. Profound dejection, unspeakable loneliness overwhelmed her. A passionate, unformulated appeal, so intense that it resembled a prayer, went out from the centre of her being to the indifferent universe. No lighted window showed itself in the darkness. The tall elms murmured with a menacing and primeval sound.

Clutching her bag and convulsively pressing her fingers upon it, she walked slowly, with uncertain steps, away from the empty house.

XII

THE seven great yews in Stone churchyard flowed upwards like blackish flames. Because it was April they had put on their decoration of small gilded shoots which they had worn every spring for three or four hundred years. The golden cypress that Clare had loved as a child had also adorned itself with new fronds curling as elegantly as the tips of dyed ostrich feathers. The sky was a dazzling field of porcelain blue across which an aerial army marched with its many banners, some milky white, some opalescent, some dark as thunder. One of these black pennons covered the sun, and at once the little churchyard seemed desolate, the flowers fluttered forlornly on the new grave. The few mourners who had attended the burial service began to shiver and move away, turning up their coat collars and thinking about the treacherous east wind.

Isabel Bonham stood apart near the plain granite cross marking her father's tomb. She did not want anyone to notice her or speak to her. Her eyes were quite dry, but tragedy filled her heart. Her heart was no longer in the world that was just putting on its spring dress, but underground, buried in the cold earth with those she had loved.

Her mind penetrated the flower-covered mound beneath which Clare lay. Lamentable visions accompanied it. 'If only I had been there! If only I hadn't gone to the north ...' her mind lamented, in the futile self-accusation of despair. The flowers blew about disconsolately in the cold wind. Already the hot-house blossoms seemed to be wilting. By to-morrow they would be windbroken, brown and limp, a pitiful mass of decay.

The mourners had gone out of sight. Isabel was alone. Slowly she turned away from the grave, a plump, solitary, ageing woman, dressed all in black. The empty church-yard seemed to her full of presences. Perhaps Clare was present, and Anthony, and her father, watching her with ghostly eyes from behind the veil of the April daylight. She began to walk home, to her house in sight of the dead.

Celia paused at the lych-gate to speak to Hugh Barring-ton. She was wearing a mink coat. The wind drove tiny furrows through the soft fur.

'I keep blaming myself,' the young man was saying, 'and yet how could I possibly have guessed . . .? How could I have anticipated anything so appalling? We were so happy together . . . She always seemed calm and con-tented — '

The doctor's brow was puckered into a frown of intense, protesting bewilderment. He could not under-stand what had happened. For once in a way life, which always ran so smoothly according to his well-ordered plan, had turned round and dealt him a serious blow. He felt outraged, shaken, distraught. To Celia he looked like a large dog which had just received an unmerited and uncomprehended beating.

'You mustn't blame yourself,' she told him. 'We all realize that you weren't in the least to blame. You heard what they said — "the balance of her mind was disturbed".'

'Yes . . . yes. But I ought to have seen . . . It's all so terrible. I shan't be able to stay in Jessington now. Everyone must be talking . . . It'll ruin me. My career is finished.'

Celia shook his hand in farewell.

'No. You must be brave. You mustn't let this get you down. People will sympathize with you — not blame you. You'll see. Everything will come all right in the end.'

With an effect of triumph the sun sprang out from behind the cloud, and it was as though the landscape suddenly started to smile. Celia passed through the gate and walked towards the car in which John Sutherland was awaiting her. Small tendrils of hair escaped from under her close fitting black hat and glittered like dancing flames. Birds were singing, a shimmering haze of blossom veiled the orchards above Great Stone.

Celia drew a deep breath, lifting her face to the lovely sunshine. She felt as though a burden which she had carried for many years had at last been removed from her. In leaving the churchyard she seemed to have stepped out of a dark and gloomy room which she would never again need to enter. She felt powerful, strong, successful, at the peak of her existence. There was nothing which she could not achieve. The world, the whole excited world, infinitely wide and wonderful, full of unlimited possibilities, lay invitingly stretched out before her.

'I'm glad we're going to New York to-morrow,' she said to the man who got out of the car to meet her, smiling, and looking into his face with clear, neutral, unfocused eyes.